Walter Richard Cassels

A Reply to Dr. Lightfoot's Essays

Walter Richard Cassels

A Reply to Dr. Lightfoot's Essays

ISBN/EAN: 9783337250768

Printed in Europe, USA, Canada, Australia, Japan

Cover: Foto ©Andreas Hilbeck / pixelio.de

More available books at **www.hansebooks.com**

A REPLY

TO

DR LIGHTFOOT'S ESSAYS

BY THE AUTHOR OF

"SUPERNATURAL RELIGION"

LONDON

LONGMANS, GREEN, AND CO.

AND NEW YORK : 15 EAST 16th STREET

1889

PRINTED BY
SPOTTISWOODE AND CO., NEW-STREET SQUARE
LONDON

INTRODUCTION.

I SINCERELY rejoice that Dr. Lightfoot has recovered from his recent illness. Of this restoration the vigorous energy of the preface to his republication of the Essays on *Supernatural Religion* affords decided evidence, and I hope that no refutation of this inference at least may be possible, however little we may agree on other points.

It was natural that Dr. Lightfoot should not be averse to preserving the more serious part of these Essays, the preparation of which cost him so much time and trouble; and the republication of this portion of his reply to my volumes, giving as it does the most eloquent and attractive statement of the ecclesiastical case, must be welcome to many. I cannot but think that it has been an error of judgment and of temper, however, to have rescued from an ephemeral state of existence and conferred literary permanence on much in his present volume, which is mere personal attack on his adversary and a deliberate attempt to discredit a writer with whom he pretends to enter into serious argument. A material part of the volume is composed of such matter. I cannot congratulate him on the spirit which he has displayed. Personally I am profoundly indifferent to such attempts at detraction, and it is with heretical amusement that I contemplate the large part which purely individual and irrelevant criticism is made to play in stuffing out the proportions of orthodox argument. In the first moment of irritation, I can well understand that hard hitting, even below the belt, might be indulged in against my work by an exasperated theologian—for even a bishop is a man,—but that such attacks should not only be perpetuated, but repeated after years of calm reflection, is at once an error and a compliment for which I was not prepared. Anything to prevent readers from taking up *Supernatural Religion* : any misrepresentation to prejudice them against its statements. Elaborate literary abuse against the author is substituted for the effective arguments against his reasoning which are unhappily wanting. In the later editions of my work, I removed everything that seemed likely to irritate or to afford openings for the discussion of minor questions, irrelevant to the main subject under treatment. Whilst Dr. Lightfoot in many cases points out such alterations, he republishes his original attacks and demonstrates the disparaging purpose of his Essays by the reiterated condemnation of passages which had so little to do with the argument that they no longer exist in the complete edition of *Supernatural Religion.* Could there be more palpable evidence of the frivolous and superficial character of his objections? It is not too much to say that in no part of these Essays has Dr. Lightfoot at all seriously entered upon the fundamental proposition of

Supernatural Religion. He has elaborately criticised notes and references : he has discussed dates and unimportant details : but as to the question whether there is any evidence for miracles and the reality of alleged Divine Revelation, his volume is an absolute blank. Bampton Lecturers and distinguished apologetic writers have frankly admitted that the Christian argument must be reconstructed. They have felt the positions, formerly considered to be impregnable, crumbling away under their feet, but nothing could more forcibly expose the feebleness of the apologetic case than this volume of Dr. Lightfoot's Essays. The substantial correctness of the main conclusions of *Supernatural Religion* is rendered all the more apparent by the reply to its reasoning. The eagerness with which Dr. Lightfoot and others rush up all the side issues and turn their backs upon the more important central proposition is in the highest degree remarkable. Those who are in doubt and who have understood what the problem to be solved really is will not get any help from his volume.

The republication of these Essays, however, has almost forced upon me the necessity of likewise republishing the reply I gave at the time of their appearance. The first Essay appeared in the *Fortnightly Review*, and others followed in the preface to the sixth edition of *Supernatural Religion*, and in that and the complete edition, in notes to the portions attacked, where reply seemed necessary. I cannot hope that readers will refer to these scattered arguments, and this volume is published with the view of affording a convenient form of reference for those interested in the discussion.

I add brief notes upon those Essays which did not require separate treatment at the time, and such further
explanations as seem to me desirable for the elucidation
of my statements. Of course, the full discussion of
Dr. Lightfoot's arguments must still be sought in the
volumes of *Supernatural Religion*, but I trust that I
may have said enough here to indicate the nature of his
allegations and their bearing on my argument.

I have likewise thought it right to add the Conclusions, without any alteration, which were written for
the complete edition, when, for the first time, having
examined all the evidence, I was in a position to wind
up the case. This is all the more necessary as they
finally show the inadequacy of Dr. Lightfoot's treatment. But I have still more been moved to append
these Conclusions in order to put them within easier
reach of those who only possess the earlier editions,
which do not contain them.

Dr. Lightfoot again reproaches me with my anony-
mity. I do not think that I am open to much rebuke
for not having the courage of my opinions; but I may
distinctly say that I have always held that arguments
upon very serious subjects should be impersonal, and
neither gain weight by the possession of a distinguished
name nor lose by the want of it. I leave the Bishop
any advantage he has in his throne, and I take my stand
upon the basis of reason and not of reputation.

CONTENTS

PAGE

I. A REPLY TO DR. LIGHTFOOT'S FIRST ESSAY ON "SUPER-
NATURAL RELIGION" 1

II. THE SILENCE OF EUSEBIUS—THE IGNATIAN EPISTLES . . 40

III. POLYCARP OF SMYRNA 115

IV. PAPIAS OF HIERAPOLIS 117

V. MELITO OF SARDIS—CLAUDIUS APOLLINARIS—POLYCRATES . 129

VI. THE CHURCHES OF GAUL 139

VII. TATIAN'S "DIATESSARON" 145

VIII. CONCLUSIONS 157

INDEX 175

I.

A REPLY TO DR. LIGHTFOOT'S FIRST ESSAY ON "SUPERNATURAL RELIGION." [1]

THE function of the critic, when rightly exercised, is so important, that it is fitting that a reviewer seriously examining serious work should receive serious and respectful consideration, however severe his remarks and however unpleasant his strictures. It is scarcely possible that a man can so fully separate himself from his work as to judge fairly either of its effect as a whole or its treatment in detail; and in every undertaking of any magnitude it is almost certain that flaws and mistakes must occur, which can best be detected by those whose perception has not been dulled by continuous and over-strained application. No honest writer, however much he may wince, can feel otherwise than thankful to anyone who points out errors or mistakes which can be rectified ; and, for myself, I may say that I desire nothing more than such frankness, and the fair refutation of any arguments which may be fallacious.

Reluctant as I must ever be, therefore, to depart from the attitude of silent attention which I think should be maintained by writers in the face of criticism, or to interrupt the fair reply of an opponent, the case is somewhat different when criticism assumes the vicious tone of the Rev. Dr. Lightfoot's article upon *Supernatural*

---

[1] Originally published in the *Fortnightly Review*, January 1, 1875.

B

Religion in the December number of the "Contemporary Review." Whilst delivering severe lectures upon want of candour and impartiality, and preaching temperance and moderation, the practice of the preacher, as sometimes happens, falls very short of his precept. The example of moderation presented to me by my clerical critic does not seem to me very edifying, his impartiality does not appear to be beyond reproach, and in his tone I fail to recognise any of the ἐπιείκεια which Mr. Matthew Arnold so justly admires. I shall not emulate the spirit of that article, and I trust that I shall not scant the courtesy with which I desire to treat Dr. Lightfoot, whose ability I admire and whose position I understand. I should not, indeed, consider it necessary at present to notice his attack at all, but that I perceive the attempt to prejudice an audience and divert attention from the issues of a serious argument by general detraction. The device is far from new, and the tactics cannot be pronounced original. In religious as well as legal controversy, the threadbare maxim : " A bad case—abuse the plaintiff's attorney," remains in force ; and it is surprising how effectual the simple practice still is. If it were granted, for the sake of argument, that each slip in translation, each error in detail and each oversight in statement, with which Canon Lightfoot reproaches *Supernatural Religion* were well founded, it must be evident to any intelligent mind that the mass of such a work would not really be affected ; such flaws—and what book of the kind escapes them—which can most easily be removed, would not weaken the central argument, and after the Apologist's ingenuity has been exerted to the utmost to blacken every blot, the basis of Supernatural Religion would not be made one whit more secure. It is, however, because I recognise that, behind this skirmishing attack, there is the constant insinuation that misstatements have been detected which have "a vital bearing" upon the question at issue, arguments "wrecked" which are of serious importance, and omissions indicated which change the aspect of reasoning, that I have thought it worth my while at once to reply. I shall endeavour briefly to show that, in thus attempting to sap the strength of my position, Dr. Lightfoot has only exposed the weakness of his own. Dr. Lightfoot somewhat scornfully says that he has the "misfortune" "to dispute not a few propositions which 'most critics' are agreed in maintaining." He will probably find that "most critics," for their part, will not consider it a very great misfortune to differ from a divine who has the misfortune of differing, on so many points, from most critics.

The first and most vehement attack made upon me by Dr. Lightfoot is regarding "a highly important passage of Irenæus," containing a reference to some other and unnamed authority, in which he considers that I am "quite unconscious of the distinction between the infinitive and indicative;" a point upon which "any fairly trained schoolboy" would decide against my reasoning. I had found fault with Tischendorf in the text, and with Dr. Westcott in a note, for inserting the words "say they," and "they taught," in rendering the oblique construction of a passage whose source is in dispute, without some mark or explanation, in the total absence of the original, that these special words were supplementary and introduced by the translator. I shall speak of Tischendorf presently, and for the moment I confine myself to Dr. Westcott. Irenæus (*Adv. Haer.* v. 36, 1) makes a statement as to what "the presbyters say" regarding the joys of the Millennial kingdom, and he then proceeds (§ 2) with indirect construction, indicating a reference to some other authority than himself, to the passage in question, in which a saying similar to John xiv. 2 is introduced. This passage is claimed by Tischendorf as a quotation from the work of Papias, and is advanced in discussing the evidence of the Bishop of Hierapolis. Dr. Westcott, without any explanation, states in his text: "In addition to the Gospels of St. Matthew and St. Mark, Papias appears to have been acquainted with the Gospel of St. John;"[1] and in a note on an earlier page: "The passage quoted by Irenæus from 'the Elders' may probably be taken as a specimen of his style of interpretation;"[2] and then follows the passage in which the indirect construction receives a specific direction by the insertion of "they taught."[3] Neither Dr. Westcott nor Dr. Lightfoot makes the slightest allusion to the fact that they are almost alone in advancing this testimony, which Dr. Lightfoot describes as having "a vital bearing on the main question at issue, the date of the fourth Gospel." The reader who had not the work of Irenæus before him to estimate the justness of the ascription of this passage to Papias, and who was not acquainted with all the circumstances, and with the state of critical opinion on the point, could scarcely, on reading such statements, understand the real position of the case.

Now the facts are as follows: Routh[4] conjectured that the whole passage in Irenæus was derived from the work of Papias, and in this he was followed by Dorner,[5] who practically introduced the suggestion to the critics of Germany, with whom it found no favour, and no one whom I remember, except Tischendorf and perhaps

---

[1] *On the Canon*, p. 65.   [2] *Ibid.* p. 61, note 2.

[3] At the end of this note Dr. Westcott adds, "Indeed, from the similar mode of introducing the story of the vine, which is afterwards referred to Papias, it is reasonable to conjecture that this interpretation is one from Papias' *Exposition*."

[4] *Reliq. Sacræ*, i. p. 10 f.

[5] *Lehre Pers. Christi*, i. p 217 f., Anm. 56, p. 218, Anm. 62.

Professor Hofstede de Groot, now seriously supports
this view. Zeller,[1] in his celebrated treatise on the external testimony for the fourth Gospel, argued against
Dorner that, in spite of the indirect construction of the
passage, there is not the slightest certainty that Irenæus
did not himself interpolate the words from the fourth
Gospel, and he affirmed the fact that there is no evidence
whatever that Papias knew that work. Anger,[2] discussing the evidence of the presbyters quoted by Irenæus
in our Gospels, refers to this passage in a note with
marked doubt, saying that *fortasse* (in italics), on account
of the chiliastic tone of the passage, it may, as Routh
conjectures, be from the work of Papias ; but in the text
he points out the great caution with which these quotations from " the presbyters" should be used. He says,
" Sed in usu horum testimoniorum faciendo cautissime
versandum est, tum quod, nisi omnia, certe pleraque ab
Irenæo *memoriter* repetuntur, tum quia hic illic incertis-
simum est, utrum ipse loquatur Irenæus an presbyte-
rorum verba recitet." Meyer,[3] who refers to the passage,
remarks that it is doubtful whether these presbyters,
whom he does not connect with Papias, derived the
saying from the Gospel or from tradition. Riggenbach[4]
alludes to it merely to abandon the passage as evidence
connected with Papias, and only claims the quotation,
in an arbitrary way, as emanating from the first half of
the second century. Professor Hofstede de Groot,[5] the
translator of Tischendorf's work into Dutch, and his
warm admirer, brings forward the quotation, after him,
as either belonging to the circle of Papias or to that
Father himself. Hilgenfeld[6] distinctly separates the

---

[1] *Theol. Jahrb.* 1845, p. 593, Anm. 2; cf. 1847, p. 160, Anm. 1.
[2] *Synops. Evang.*, Proleg. xxxi.
[3] *Komm. Ev. des Johannes*, p. 6 f.   [4] *Die Zeugn. Ev. Joh.* p. 116 f.
[5] *Basilides*, p. 110 f.
[6] *Zeitschr. für wiss. Theol.* 1867, p. 186, Anm. 1, 1868, p. 219, Anm. 4;
cf. 1865, p. 334 ff., " Die Evangelien," p. 339, Anm. 4.

presbyters of this passage from Papias, and asserts that they may have lived in the second half of the second century. Luthardt,[1] in the new issue of his youthful work on the fourth Gospel, does not attempt to associate the quotation with the book of Papias, but merely argues that the presbyters to whom Irenæus was indebted for it formed a circle to which Polycarp and Papias belonged. Zahn[2] does not go beyond him in this. Dr. Davidson, while arguing that "it is impossible to show that the four (Gospels) were current as early as A.D. 150," refers to this passage, and says: "It is precarious to infer with Tischendorf either that Irenæus derived his account of the presbyters from Papias's book, or that the authority of the elders carries us back to the termination of the apostolic times;" and he concludes: "Is it not evident that Irenæus employed it (the word 'elders') loosely, without an exact idea of the persons he meant?"[3] In another place Dr. Davidson still more directly says: "The second proof is founded on a passage in Irenæus, where the Father, professing to give an account of the eschatological tradition of ' the presbyter, a disciple of the Apostles,' introduces the words, 'and that therefore the Lord said, "In my Father's house are many mansions."' Here it is equally uncertain whether a work of Papias be meant as the source of the quotation, and whether that Father did not insert something of his own, or something borrowed elsewhere, and altered according to the text of the Gospel."[4]

With these exceptions, no critic seems to have considered it worth his while to refer to this passage at all. Neither in considering the external evidences for the

---

[1] *Der Johann. Ursprung des viert. Evang.* 1874, p. 72.
[2] *Th. Stud. u. Krit.* 1866, p. 674.   [3] *Intro. N. T.* ii. p. 424 f.
[4] *Ibid.* ii. p. 372.

antiquity of the fourth Gospel, nor in discussing the question whether Papias was acquainted with it, do apologetic writers like Bleek, Ebrard, Olshausen, Guericke, Kirchhofer, Thiersch, or Tholuck, or impartial writers like Credner, De Wette, Gfrörer, Lücke, and others commit the mistake of even alluding to it, although many of them directly endeavour to refute the article of Zeller, in which it is cited and rejected, and all of them point out so indirect an argument for his knowledge of the Gospel as the statement of Eusebius that Papias made use of the first Epistle of John. Indeed, on neither side is the passage introduced into the controversy at all; and whilst so many conclude positively that Papias was not acquainted with the fourth Gospel, the utmost that is argued by the majority of apologetic critics is, that his ignorance of it is not actually proved. Those who go further and urge the supposed use of the Epistle as testimony in favour of his also knowing the Gospel would only too gladly have produced this passage, if they could have maintained it as taken from the work of Papias. It would not be permissible to assume that any of the writers to whom we refer were ignorant of the existence of the passage, because they are men thoroughly acquainted with the subject generally, and most of them directly refer to the article of Zeller in which the quotation is discussed.

This is an instance in which Dr. Lightfoot has the "misfortune to dispute not a few propositions, which most critics are agreed in maintaining." I have no objection to his disputing anything. All that I suggest as desirable in such a case is some indication that there is anything in dispute, which, I submit, general readers could scarcely discover from the statements of Dr. Westcott or the remarks of Dr. Lightfoot. Now in regard to myself, in desiring to avoid what I objected to in others, I may have gone to the other extreme. But although I perhaps too carefully avoided any indication as to who says "that there is this distinction of dwelling," &c., I did what was possible to attract attention to the actual indirect construction, a fact which must have been patent, as Dr. Lightfoot says, to a "fairly trained schoolboy." I doubly indicated, by a mark, and by adding a note, the commencement of the sentence, and not only gave the original below, but actually inserted in the text the opening words, εἶναι δὲ τὴν διαστολὴν ταύτην τῆς οἰκήσεως, for the express purpose of showing the construction. That I did not myself mistake the point is evident, not only from this, but from the fact that I do not make any objection to the translations of Tischendorf and Dr. Westcott, beyond condemning the *unmarked* introduction of precise words, and that I proceed to argue that "the presbyters," to whom the passage is referred, are in no case necessarily to be associated with the work of Papias, which would have been mere waste of time had I intended to maintain that Irenæus quoted direct from the Gospel. An observation made to me regarding my note on Dr. Westcott, showed me that I had been misunderstood, and led me to refer to the place again. I immediately withdrew the note which had been interpreted in a way very different from what I had intended, and at the same time perceiving that my argument was obscure and liable to the misinterpretation of which Dr. Lightfoot has made such eager use, I myself at once recast it as well as I could within the limits at my command,[1] and this was already published before Dr. Lightfoot's criticism appeared, and before I had any knowledge of his articles.[2]

[1] The work was all printed, and I could only reprint the sheet with such alterations as could be made by omissions and changes at the part itself.

[2] Dr. Lightfoot makes use of my second edition.

With regard to Tischendorf, however, the validity of my objection is practically admitted in the fullest way by Dr. Lightfoot himself. "Tischendorf's words," he says, " are ' und deshalb, sagen sie, habe der Herr den Ausspruch gethan.' He might have spared the ' sagen sie,' because the German idiom ' habe' enables him to express the main fact that the words were not Irenæus's own without this addition." Writing of a brother apologist of course he apologetically adds : " But he has not altered any idea which the original contains." I affirm, on the contrary, that he has very materially altered an idea—that, in fact, he has warped the whole argument, for Dr. Lightfoot has mercifully omitted to point out that the words just quoted are introduced by the distinct assertion " that Irenæus quotes even out of the mouth of the presbyters, those high authorities of Papias." The German apologist, therefore, not giving the original text, not saying a word of the adverse judgment of most critics, after fully rendering the construction of Irenæus by the " habe," quietly inserts " say they," in reference to these " high authorities of Papias," without a hint that these words are his own.[2]

My argument briefly is, that there is no ground for asserting that the passage in question, with its reference to " many mansions," was derived from the presbyters of Papias, or from his book, and that it is not a quotation from a work which quotes the presbyters as quoting these words, but one made more directly by Irenæus— not directly from the Gospel, but probably from some contemporary, and representing nothing more than the exegesis of his own day.

The second point of Canon Lightfoot's attack is in

---

[1] *Contemporary Review*, December, p. 4, n. 1 ; *Essays on S. R.* p. 4, n. 4.
[2] Professor Hofstede de Groot, in advancing this passage after the example of Tischendorf, carefully distinguishes the words which he introduces, referring it to the presbyters, by placing them within brackets.

connection with a discussion of the date of Celsus. Dr. Lightfoot quotes a passage from Origen given in my work,[1] upon which he comments as follows: " On the strength of the passage so translated, our author supposes that Origen's impression concerning the date of Celsus had meanwhile been ' considerably modified,' and remarks that he now ' treats him as a contemporary.' Unfortunately, however, the tenses, on which everything depends, are freely handled in this translation. Origen does not say ' Celsus *has promised*,' but ' Celsus *promises* ' (ἐπαγγελλόμενον)—*i.e.*, in the treatise before him, Origen's knowledge was plainly derived from the book itself. And, again, he does not say ' If he *has not fulfilled* his promise to write,' but ' If he *did not write* as he undertook to do ' (ἔγραψεν ὑποσχόμενος) ; nor ' If he *has commenced and finished*,' but ' If he *commenced and finished* ' (ἀρξάμενος συνετέλεσε). Thus Origen's language itself here points to a past epoch, and is in strict accordance with the earlier passages in his work."[2] These remarks, and the triumphant exclamation of Dr. Lightfoot at the close that here " an elaborate argument is wrecked on this rock of grammar," convey a totally wrong impression of the case.

The argument regarding this passage in Origen occurs in a controversy between Tischendorf and Volkmar, the particulars of which I report;[3] and to avoid anticipation of the point, I promise to give the passage in its place, which I subsequently do. All the complimentary observations which Dr. Lightfoot makes upon the translation actually fall upon the head of his brother apologist, Tischendorf, whose rendering, as he so much insists upon it, I merely reproduce. The manner in which Tischendorf attacks Volkmar in connection with

---

[1] *S. R.* ii. p. 231 f. [2] *Contemporary Review*, December, p. 5 f.; *Essays on S. R.* p. 7. [3] *S. R.* ii. 228 ff.

this passage forcibly reminds me of the amenities addressed to myself by Dr. Lightfoot, who seems unconsciously to have caught the trick of his precursor's scolding. Volkmar had paraphrased Origen's words in a way of which his critic disapproved, and Tischendorf comments as follows : " But here again we have to do with nothing else than a completely abortive fabrication, a certificate of our said critic's poverty. For the assertion derived from the close of the work of Origen rests upon gross ignorance or upon intentional deception. The words of Origen to his patron Ambrosius, who had prompted him to the composition of the whole apology, run as follows " [and here I must give the German] : " ' Wenn dass Celsus versprochen hat ' [*has promised*] ' (jedenfalls in seinem gegen das Christenthum gerichteten und von Origenes widerlegten Buche) noch eine andere Schrift nach dieser zu verfassen, worin u.s.w.' ' Wenn er nun diese zweite Schrift trotz seines Versprechens nicht geschrieben hat ' [*has not written*], ' so genügt es uns mit diesen acht Büchern auf seine Schrift geantwortet zu haben. Wenn er aber auch jene unternommen und vollendet hat ' [*has undertaken and completed*], ' so treib das Buch auf und schicke es, damit wir auch darauf antworten,' " &c.[1] Now this translation of Tischendorf is not made carelessly, but deliberately, for the express purpose of showing the actual words of Origen, and correcting the version of Volkmar ; and he insists upon these tenses not only by referring to the Greek of these special phrases, but by again contrasting with them the paraphrase of Volkmar.[2] Whatever disregard of tenses and " free handling " of Origen there

[1] *Wann wurden*, u.s.w., p. 73 f.
[2] The translation in Scholten's work is substantially the same as Tischendorf's, except that he has " promises " for " has promised," which is of no importance. Upon this, however, Scholten argues that Celsus is treated as a contemporary.

may be here, therefore, are due to Tischendorf, who may be considered as good a scholar as Dr. Lightfoot, and not a less zealous apologist.

Instead of depending on the " strength of the passage so translated," however, as Canon Lightfoot represents, my argument is independent of this or any other version of Origen's words ; and, in fact, the point is only incidentally introduced, and more as the view of others than my own. I point out[1] that Origen evidently knows nothing of his adversary : and I add that " it is almost impossible to avoid the conviction that, during the time he was composing his work, his impressions concerning the date and identity of his opponent became considerably modified." I then proceed to enumerate some of the reasons. In the earlier portion of his first book (i. 8), Origen has heard that his Celsus is the Epicurean of the reign of Hadrian and later, but a little further on (i. 68), he confesses his ignorance as to whether he is the same Celsus who wrote against magic, which Celsus the Epicurean actually did. In the fourth book (iv. 36) he expresses uncertainty as to whether the Epicurean Celsus had composed the work against Christians which he is refuting, and at the close of his treatise he treats him as a contemporary, for, as I again mention, Volkmar and others assert, on the strength of the passage in the eighth book and from other considerations, that Celsus really was a contemporary of Origen. I proceed to argue that, even if Celsus were the Epicurean friend of Lucian, there could be no ground for assigning to him an early date ; but, on the contrary, that so far from being an Epicurean, the Celsus attacked by Origen evidently was a Neo-Platonist. This, and the circumstance that his work indicates a period of persecution against Christians, leads to the conclusion, I

---

[1] *S. R.* ii. p. 220 ff.

point out, that he must be dated about the beginning of the third century. My argument, in short, scarcely turns upon the passage in Origen at all, and that which renders it incapable of being wrecked is the fact that Celsus never mentions the Gospels, and much less adds anything to our knowledge of their authors, which can entitle them to greater credit as witnesses for the reality of Divine Revelation.

I do not intend to bandy many words with Canon Lightfoot regarding translations. Nothing is so easy as to find fault with the rendering of passages from another language, or to point out variations in tenses and expressions, not in themselves of the slightest importance to the main issue, in freely transferring the spirit of sentences from their natural context to an isolated position in quotation. Such a personal matter as Dr. Lightfoot's general strictures, in this respect, I feel cannot interest the readers of this Review. I am quite ready to accept correction even from an opponent where I am wrong, but I am quite content to leave to the judgment of all who will examine them in a fair spirit the voluminous quotations in my work. The 'higher criticism,' in which Dr. Lightfoot seems to have indulged in this article, scarcely rises above the correction of an exercise or the conjugation of a verb.[1]

---

[1] I may here briefly refer to one or two instances of translation attacked by Dr. Lightfoot. He sneers at such a rendering as ὁ λόγος ἐδήλου, " Scripture declares," introducing an isolated phrase from Justin Martyr (ii. 296). The slight liberty taken with the tense is surely excusable in such a case, and for the rest I may point out that Prudentius Maranus renders the words " . . . . scripturam declarare," and Otto " . . . . effatum declarare." They occur in reference to passages from the Old Testament quoted in controversy with a Jew. The next passage is κατὰ κόρρης προπηλακίζειν, which Dr. Lightfoot says is rendered " to inflict a blow on one side," but this is not the case. The phrase occurs in contrasting the words of Matt. v. 39, ἀλλ' ὅστις σε ῥαπίσει ἐπὶ τὴν δεξιάν σου σιαγόνα, στρέψον αὐτῷ καὶ τὴν ἄλλην, with a passage in Athenagoras, ἀλλὰ τοῖς μὲν κἂν κατὰ κόρρης προσπηλακίζωσι, καὶ τὸ ἕτερον παίειν παρέχειν τῆς κεφαλῆς μέρος. In endeavouring to convey to the English reader some idea of the linguistic difference, I rendered the latter (ii. 193), " but to those who inflict a blow on the one side, also to present

I am extremely obliged to Dr. Lightfoot for pointing out two clerical errors which had escaped me, but which have been discovered and magnified by his microscopic criticism, and thrown at my head by his apologetic zeal.   The first is in reference to what he describes as " a highly important question of Biblical criticism."   In speaking, *en passant*, of a passage in John v. 3, 4, in connection with the " Age of Miracles," the words " it is argued that " were accidentally omitted from vol. i. p. 113, line 19, and the sentence should read, " and it is argued that it was probably a later interpolation." [1]   In vol. ii. p. 420, after again mentioning the rejection of the passage, I proceed to state my own personal belief that the words must have originally stood in the text, because v. 7 indicates the existence of such a context.   The second error is in vol. ii. p. 423, line 24, in which "only" has been substituted for "never" in deciphering my MS.   Since this is such a *commonplace* of " apologists," as Dr. Lightfoot points out, surely he might have put a courteous construction upon the error, instead of venting upon me so much righteous indignation.   I can assure him that I do not in the

---

the other side, *of the head*," &c., inserting the three Greek words after " side," to explain the suspension of sense, and the merging, for the sake of brevity, the double expression in the words I have italicised.   Dr. Lightfoot represents the phrase as ending at " side."   The passage from Tertullian was quoted almost solely for the purpose of showing the uncertainty, in so bold a writer, of the expression " videtur," for which reason, although the Latin is given below, the word was introduced into the text.   It was impossible for anyone to *mistake* the tense and meaning of " quem cœderet," but I ventured to paraphase the words and their context, instead of translating them.   In this sentence, I may say, the " mutilation hypothesis " is introduced, and thereafter Tertullian proceeds to press against Marcion his charge of mutilating the Gospel of Luke, and I desired to contrast the doubt of the " videtur " with the assurance of the subsequent charge.   I had imagined that no one could have doubted that Luke is represented as one of the " Commentatores."

[1] I altered " certainly " to " probably " in the second edition, as Dr. Lightfoot points out, in order to avoid the possibility of exaggeration ; but my mind was so impressed with the certainty that I had clearly shown I was merely, for the sake of fairness, reporting the critical judgment of others, that I did not perceive the absence of the words given above.

slightest degree grudge him the full benefit of the argument that the fourth Gospel never once distinguishes John the Baptist from the Apostle John by the addition ὁ βαπτιστής.[1]

I turn, however, to a more important matter. Canon Lightfoot attacks me in no measured terms for a criticism upon Dr. Westcott's mode of dealing with a piece of information regarding Basilides. He says—

"Dr. Westcott writes of Basilides as follows :—

"'At the same time he appealed to the authority of Glaucias, who, as well as St. Mark, was "an interpreter of St. Peter."' ('Canon,' p. 264.)

"The inverted commas are given here as they appear in Dr. Westcott's book. It need hardly be said that Dr. Westcott is simply illustrating the statement of Basilides that Glaucias was an interpreter of St. Peter by the similar statement of Papias and others that St. Mark was an interpreter of the same apostle—a very innocent piece of information, one would suppose. On this passage, however, our author remarks—

"'Now we have here again an illustration of the same misleading system which we have already condemned, and shall further refer to, in the introduction after "Glaucias" of the words "*who, as well as St. Mark, was* an interpreter of St. Peter." The words in italics are the gratuitous addition of Canon Westcott himself, and can only have been inserted for one of two purposes—(1) to assert the fact that Glaucias was actually an interpreter of Peter, as tradition represented Mark to be ; or (2) to insinuate to unlearned readers that Basilides himself acknowledged Mark as well as Glaucias as the interpreter of Peter. We can hardly suppose the first to have been the intention, and we regret to be forced back upon the second, and infer that the temptation to weaken the inferences from the appeal of Basilides to the uncanonical Glaucias, by coupling with it the allusion to Mark, was, unconsciously, no doubt, too strong for the apologist.' ('S. R.' i. p. 459.)

---

[1] Dr. Lightfoot is mistaken in his ingenious conjecture of my having been misled by the "nur" of Credner ; but so scrupulous a critic might have mentioned that I not only refer to Credner for this argument, but also to *De Wette*, who has, ". . . . dass er *nic* Joh. dem Täufer wie der Synoptiker den Beinamen ὁ βαπτιστής giebt" (*Einl. N. T.* p. 230), and to *Bleek*, who says, "nicht ein einziges Mal" (*Beiträge*, p. 178, and *Einl. N. T.* p. 150), which could not be misread.

"Dr. Westcott's honour may safely be left to take care of itself. It stands far too high to be touched by insinuations like these. I only call attention to the fact that our author has removed Dr. Westcott's inverted commas, and then founded on the passage so manipulated a charge of unfair dealing, which could only be sustained in their absence, and which even then no one but himself would have thought of."[1]

In order to make this matter clear, I must venture more fully to quote Dr. Westcott's statements regarding Basilides.   Dr. Westcott says : "Since Basilides lived on the verge of the Apostolic times, it is not surprising that he made use of other sources of Christian doctrine besides the canonical books.   The belief in Divine Inspiration was still fresh and real ; and Eusebius relates that he set up imaginary prophets, Barcabbas and Barcoph (Parchor)—'names to strike terror into the superstitious'—by whose writings he supported his peculiar views.   At the same time he appealed to the authority of Glaucias, who, as well as St. Mark, was 'an interpreter of St. Peter;'[2] and he also made use of certain 'Traditions of Matthias,' which claimed to be grounded on 'private intercourse with the Saviour.'[3] It appears, moreover, that he himself published a gospel—a 'Life of Christ,' as it would perhaps be called in our days, or 'The Philosophy of Christianity'—but he admitted the historic truth of all the facts contained in the canonical gospels, and used them as Scripture. For, in spite of his peculiar opinions, the testimony of Basilides to our 'acknowledged' books is comprehensive and clear.   In the few pages of his writings which remain, there are certain references to the Gospels of St. Matthew, St. Luke, and St. John, &c."   And in a

---

[1] *Contemporary Review*, December, p. 15; *Essays on S. R.* p. 21 f.
[2] Clem. Alex. *Strom.* vii. 17–106.   Dr. Westcott gives the above reference, but does not quote the passage.
[3] Dr. Westcott quotes the passage relative to Matthias.

note Dr. Westcott adds, "The following examples will be sufficient to show his mode of quotation, &c." [1]

Not a word of qualification or doubt is added to these extraordinary statements, for a full criticism of which I must beg the reader to be good enough to refer to *Supernatural Religion*, ii. pp. 41–54. Setting aside here the important question as to what the "gospel" of Basilides—to which Dr. Westcott gives the fanciful names of a "Life of Christ," or "Philosophy of Christianity," without a shadow of evidence—really was, it could scarcely be divined, for instance, that the statement that Basilides "admitted the historic truth of all the facts contained in the canonical gospels" rests solely upon a sentence in the work attributed to Hippolytus, to the effect that, after his generation, all things regarding the Saviour—according to the *followers* of Basilides—occurred in the same way as they are written in the Gospels. Again, it could scarcely be supposed by an ordinary reader that the assertion that Basilides used the "canonical gospels"—there certainly were no "canonical" gospels in his day—"as Scripture," that his testimony "to our 'acknowledged' books is comprehensive and clear," and that "in the few pages of his writings which remain there are certain references" to those gospels, which show "his method of quotation," is not based upon any direct extracts from his writings, but solely upon passages in an epitome by Hippolytus of the views of the school of Basilides, not ascribed directly to Basilides himself, but introduced by a mere indefinite $\phi\eta\sigma\iota$.[2] Why, I might enquire in the vein of Dr. Lightfoot, is not a syllable said of all this, or of the fact, which completes the separation of these passages from Basilides, that the Gnosticism described by Hippo-

---

[1] *Canon*, p. 255 f.
[2] The same remarks apply to the two passages, pointed out by Tischendorf, from Clement of Alexandria and Epiphanius.

lytus is not that of Basilides, but clearly of a later type; and that writers of that period, and notably Hippolytus himself, were in the habit of putting, as it might seem, by the use of an indefinite "he says," sentiments into the mouth of the founder of a sect which were only expressed by his later followers?   As Dr. Lightfoot evidently highly values the testimony of Luthardt, I will quote the words of that staunch apologist to show that, in this, I do not merely represent the views of a hetero-dox school.   In discussing the supposed quotations from the fourth Gospel, which Dr. Westcott represents as "certain references" to it by Basilides himself, Luthardt says : "But to this is opposed the considera-tion that, as we know from Irenæus, &c., the original system of Basilides had a dualistic character, whilst that of the 'Philosophumena' is pantheistic. We must recognise that Hippolytus, in the 'Philosophumena,' not unfrequently makes the founder of a sect responsible for that which in the first place concerns his disciples, so that from these quotations only the use of the Johannine Gospel in the school of Basilides is un-doubtedly proved, but not on the part of the founder himself." [1]

It is difficult to recognise in this fancy portrait the Basilides regarding whom a large body of eminent critics conclude that he did not know our Gospels at all, but made use of an uncanonical work, supplemented by traditions from Glaucias and Matthias ; but, as if the heretic had not been sufficiently restored to the odour of sanctity, the additional touch is given in the passage more immediately before us.   Dr. Westcott conveys the information contained in the single sentence of Clement of Alexandria, καθάπερ ὁ Βασιλείδης κἂν Γλαυκίαν ἐπιγράφηται διδάσκαλον, ὡς αὐχοῦσιν αὐτοί, τὸν Πέτρου

[1] Luthardt, *Der Johann. Ursprung des viert. Evang.* 1874, p. 85 f.

ἑρμηνέα,[1] in the following words ; and I quote the state-ment exactly as it has stood in my text from the very first, in order to show the inverted commas upon which Dr. Lightfoot lays so much stress as having been re-moved. In mentioning this fact Canon Westcott says : "At the same time he appealed to the authority of Glaucias, who, as well as St. Mark, was ' an inter-preter of St. Peter.'[2] Now we have here, again, an illustration," &c. ; and then follows the passage quoted by Dr. Lightfoot. The positive form given to the words of Clement, and the introduction of the words " as well as St. Mark," seem at once to impart a full flavour of orthodoxy to Basilides which I do not find in the original. I confess that I fail to see any special virtue in the inverted commas ; but as Dr. Lightfoot does, let me point out to him that he commences his quotation—upon the strength of which he accuses me of " manipu-lating " a passage, and then founding upon it a charge of unfair dealing—immediately after the direct citation from Dr. Westcott's work, in which those inverted commas are given. The words they mark are a quota-tion from Clement, and in my re-quotation a few lines lower down they are equally well indicated by being the only words not put in italics. The fact is, that Dr. Lightfoot has mistaken and misstated the whole case. He has been so eagerly looking for the mote in my eye that he has failed to perceive the beam which is in his own eye. It is by this wonderful illustration that he " exemplifies the elaborate looseness which pervades the critical portion of this (my) book."[3] It rather exem-plifies the uncritical looseness which pervades his own article.

Dr. Lightfoot says, and says rightly, that " Dr. West-

---

[1] *Strom.* vii. 17, § 106. [2] *Canon,* p. 255.
[3] *Contemporary Review,* December, p. 16 [*Essays,* p. 22].

cott's honour may safely be left to take care of itself." It would have been much better to have left it to take care of itself, indeed, than trouble it by such advocacy. If anything could check just or generous expression, it would be the tone adopted by Dr. Lightfoot; but nevertheless I again say, in the most unreserved manner, that neither in this instance nor in any other have I had the most distant intention of attributing "corrupt motives" to a man like Dr. Westcott, whose single-mindedness I recognise, and for whose earnest character I feel genuine respect. The utmost that I have at any time intended to point out is that, utterly possessed as he is by orthodox views in general, and of the canon in particular, he sees facts, I consider, through a dogmatic medium, and unconsciously imparts his own peculiar colouring to statements which should be more impartially made.

Dr. Lightfoot will not even give me credit for fairly stating the arguments of my adversaries. "The author," he says, "does indeed single out from time to time the weaker arguments of 'apologetic' writers, and on these he dwells at great length; but their weightier facts and lines of reasoning are altogether ignored by him, though they often occur in the same books, and even in the same contexts which he quotes."[1] I am exceedingly indebted to Dr. Lightfoot for having had compassion upon my incapacity to distinguish these arguments, and for giving me "samples" of the "weightier facts and lines of reasoning" of apologists which I have ignored.

The first of these with which he favours me is in connection with an anachronism in the epistle ascribed to Polycarp, Ignatius being spoken of in chapter thirteen as living, and information requested regarding him "and those who are with him;" whereas in an earlier passage he is represented as dead. Dr. Lightfoot reproaches

[1] *Contemporary Review*, December, p. 8 [*ibid.* p. 11].

me :—" Why, then, does he not notice the answer which he might have found in any common source of information, that when the Latin version (the Greek is wanting here) 'de his qui cum eo sunt' is re-translated into the original language, τοῖς σὺν αὐτῷ the 'anachronism' altogether disappears?"[1] As Dr. Lightfoot does not apparently attach much weight to my replies, I venture to give my reasons for not troubling my readers with this argument in words which, I hope, may find more favour with him. Dr. Donaldson, in his able work on "Christian Literature and Doctrine," says : "In the ninth chapter Ignatius is spoken of as a martyr, an example to the Philippians of patience. . . . In the thirteenth chapter Polycarp requests information with regard to 'Ignatius and those with him.' These words occur only in the Latin translation of the epistle. To get rid of the difficulty which they present, it has been supposed that the words 'de his qui cum eo sunt' are a wrong rendering of the Greek περὶ τῶν μετ᾽ αὐτοῦ. And then the words are supposed to mean, 'concerning Ignatius (of whose death I heard, but of which I wish particulars) and those who *were* with him.' But even the Greek could not be forced into such a meaning as this ; and, moreover, there is no reason to impugn the Latin translation, except the peculiar difficulty presented by a comparison with the ninth chapter."[2] Dr. Lightfoot, however, does impugn it. It is apparently his habit to impugn translations. He accuses the ancient Latin translator of freely handling the tenses of a Greek text which the critic himself has never seen. Here it is Dr. Lightfoot's argument which is " wrecked upon this rock of grammar."

The next example of the " weightier facts and lines

---

[1] *Contemporary Review*, p. 8 [*ibid.* p. 11].
[2] *A Crit. History of Chr. Lit. and Doctrine*, i. 184 f. I do not refer to the numerous authors who enforce this view.

of reasoning" of apologists which I have ignored is as
follows :—

> "Again, when he devotes more than forty pages to the discussion
> of Papias, why does he not even mention the view maintained by Dr.
> Westcott and others (and certainly suggested by a strict interpreta-
> tion of Papias' own words), that this father's object, in his ' Exposi-
> tion,' was not to construct a new evangelical narrative, but to in-
> terpret and to illustrate by oral tradition one already lying before
> him in written documents ? This view, if correct, entirely alters the
> relation of Papias to the written Gospels ; and its discussion was a
> matter of essential importance to the main question at issue."[1]

I reply that the object of my work was not to discuss views advanced without a shadow of evidence, contradicted by the words of Papias himself, and absolutely
incapable of proof. My object was the much more
practical and direct one of ascertaining whether Papias
affords any evidence with regard to our Gospels which
could warrant our believing in the occurrence of miraculous events for which they are the principal testimony. Even if it could be proved, which it cannot be,
that Papias actually had "written documents" before
him, the cause of our Gospels would not be one jot
advanced, inasmuch as it could not be shown that these
documents were our Gospels; and the avowed preference of Papias for tradition over books, so clearly expressed, implies anything but respect for any written
documents with which he was acquainted. However
important such a discussion may appear to Dr. Lightfoot in the absence of other evidence, it is absolutely
devoid of value in an enquiry into the reality of Divine
Revelation.

The next " sample " of these ignored "weightier facts
and lines of reasoning" given by Dr. Lightfoot is the
following :—

> "Again, when he reproduces the Tübingen fallacy respecting

' the strong prejudice' of Hegesippus against St. Paul, and quotes the often-quoted passage from Stephanus Gobarus, in which this writer refers to the language of Hegesippus condemning the use of the words, 'Eye hath not seen,' &c., why does he not state that these words were employed by heretical teachers to justify their rites of initiation, and consequently 'apologetic' writers contend that Hegesippus refers to the words, not as used by St. Paul, but as misapplied by these heretics? Since, according to the Tübingen interpretation, this single notice contradicts everything else which we know of the opinions of Hegesippus, the view of 'apologists' might, perhaps, have been worth a moment's consideration." [1]

I reply, why does this punctilious objector omit to point out that I merely mention the anti-Pauline interpretation incidentally in a single sentence,[2] and after a few words as to the source of the quotation in Cor. if. 9, I proceed: "This, however, does not concern us here, and we have merely to examine ' the saying of the Lord,' which Hegesippus opposes to the passage, 'Blessed are your eyes,' " &c., this being, in fact, the sole object of my quotation from Stephanus Gobarus? Why does he not also state that I distinctly refer to Tischendorf's denial that Hegesippus was opposed to Paul? And why does he not further state that, instead of being the " single notice " from which the view of the anti-Pauline feelings of Hegesippus is derived, that conclusion is based upon the whole tendency of the fragments of his writings which remain? It was not my purpose to enter into any discussion of the feeling against Paul entertained by a large section of the early Church. What I have to say upon that subject will appear in my examination of the Acts of the Apostles.

"And again," says Dr. Lightfoot, proceeding with his samples of ignored weightier lines of reasoning,

"in the elaborate examination of Justin Martyr's evangelical quotations . . . . our author frequently refers to Dr. Westcott's book to censure it, and many comparatively insignificant points are

---

[1] *Contemporary Review*, p. 8 f. [*ibid.* p. 11].　　[2] *S. R.* i. p. 441.

discussed at great length. Why, then, does he not once mention Dr. Westcott's argument founded on the looseness of Justin Martyr's quotations from the Old Testament as throwing some light on the degree of accuracy which he might be expected to show in quoting the Gospels? A reader fresh from the perusal of *Supernatural Religion* will have his eyes opened as to the character of Justin's mind when he turns to Dr. Westcott's book, and finds how Justin interweaves, misnames, and misquotes passages from the Old Testament. It cannot be said that these are unimportant points." [1]

Now the fact is, that in the first 105 pages of my examination of Justin Martyr I do not once refer in my text to Dr. Westcott's work; and when I finally do so it is for the purposes of discussing what seemed to me a singular argument, demanding a moment's attention.[2] Dr. Westcott, whilst maintaining that Justin's quotations are derived from our Gospels, argues that only in seven passages out of the very numerous citations in his writings " does Justin profess to give the exact words recorded in the 'Memoirs.' "[3] The reason why I do not feel it at all necessary to discuss the other views of Dr. Westcott here mentioned is practically given in the final sentence of a note quoted by Dr. Lightfoot,[4] which sentence he has thought it right to omit. The note is as follows, and the sentence to which I refer I put in italics: " For the arguments of apologetic criticism, the reader may be referred to Canon Westcott's work 'On the Canon,' pp. 112–139. Dr. Westcott does not attempt to deny the fact that Justin's quotations are different from the text of our Gospels, but he accounts for his variations on grounds which are purely imaginary. *It is evident that so long as there are such variations to be explained away, at least no proof of identity is possible.*"[5] It will be observed

---

[1] *Contemporary Review*, p. 8 f. [*ibid.* p. 12 f.]   [2] *S. R.* i. p. 387 ff.
[3] *Canon*, p. 112 f.   [4] *Contemporary Review*, p. 9, note [*ibid.* p. 12. n. 4].
[5] *S. R.* i. p. 360, note 1. Dr. Lightfoot, of course, " can hardly suppose " that " I had read the passage to which I refer."

that although I do not discuss Dr. Westcott's views, I pointedly refer those who desire to know what the arguments on the other side are to his work. Let me repeat, once for all, that my object in examining the writings of the Fathers is not to form theories and conjectures as to what documents they may possibly have used, but to ascertain whether they afford any positive evidence regarding our existing Gospels, which can warrant our believing, upon their authority, the miraculous contents of Christianity. Any argument that, although Justin, for instance, never once names any of our Gospels, and out of very numerous quotations of sayings of Jesus very rarely indeed quotes anything which has an exact parallel in those Gospels, yet he may have made use of our Gospels, because he also frequently misquotes passages from the Old Testament, is worthless for the purpose of establishing the reality of Divine Revelation. From the point of view of such an enquiry, I probably go much further into the examination of Justin's "Memoirs" than was at all necessary.

Space, however, forbids my further dwelling on these instances, regarding which Dr. Lightfoot says: "In every instance which I have selected"—and to which I have replied—"these omitted considerations vitally affect the main question at issue." [1] If Dr. Lightfoot had devoted half the time to mastering what "the main question at issue" really is, which he has wasted in finding minute faults in me, he might have spared himself the trouble of giving these instances at all. If such considerations have vital importance, the position of the question may easily be understood. Dr. Lightfoot, however, evidently seems to suppose that I can be charged with want of candour and of fulness, because I do not reproduce every shred and tatter of apologetic

---

[1] *Contemporary Review*, p. 9 [*ibid.* p. 13].

reasoning which divines continue to flaunt about after others have rejected them as useless. He again accuses me, in connection with the fourth Gospel, of systematically ignoring the arguments of " apologetic " writers, and he represents my work as " the very reverse of full and impartial." " Once or twice, indeed," he says, " he fastens on passages from such writers, that he may make capital of them ; but their main arguments remain wholly unnoticed." [1] I confess that I find it somewhat difficult to distinguish between those out of which I am said to " make capital " and those which Dr. Lightfoot characterises as " their main arguments," if I am to judge by the " samples " of them which he gives me. For instance,[2] he asks why, when asserting that the Synoptics clearly represent the ministry of Jesus as having been limited to a single year, and his preaching as confined to Galilee and Jerusalem, whilst the fourth Gospel distributes the teaching of Jesus between Galilee, Samaria, and Jerusalem, makes it extend over three years, and refers to three passovers spent by Jesus at Jerusalem :

" Why then," he asks,

" does he not add that 'apologetic' writers refer to such passages as Matt. xiii. 37 (comp. Luke xiii. 34), 'O Jerusalem, Jerusalem . . . . how often would I have gathered thy children together'? Here the expression 'how often,' it is contended, obliges us to postulate other visits, probably several visits, to Jerusalem, which are not recorded in the Synoptic Gospels themselves. And it may be suggested also that the twice-repeated notice of time in the context of St. Luke, 'I do cures to-day and to-morrow, and the third day I

[1] *Contemporary Review,* p. 9 [*ibid.* p. 13].

[2] I cannot go through every instance, but I may briefly say that such a passage as "Ye are of your father the devil" and the passage Matt. xi. 27 *seq.* are no refutation whatever of my statement of the contrast between the fourth Gospel and the Synoptics ; and that the allusion to Paul's teaching in the Apocalypse is in no way excluded even by his death. Regarding the relations between Paul and the " pillar " Apostles, I hope to speak hereafter. I must maintain that my argument regarding the identification of an eye-witness (ii. p. 444 ff.) sufficiently meets the reasoning to which Dr. Lightfoot refers.

shall be perfected,' 'I must walk *to-day and to-morrow and the day following*,' points to the very duration of our Lord's ministry, as indicated by the fourth Gospel. If so, the coincidence is the more remarkable because it does not appear that St. Luke himself, while recording these prophetic words, was aware of their full historical import." [1]

Now it might have struck Dr. Lightfoot that if any-one making an enquiry into the reality of Divine Reve-lation were obliged, in order to escape charges of want of candour, fulness, and impartiality, or insinuations of ignorance, to reproduce and refute all apologetic argu-ments like this, the duration of modern life would scarcely suffice for the task; and "if they should be written every one, I suppose that even the world itself could not contain all the books that should be written." It is very right that anyone believing it valid should advance this or any other reasoning in reply to objec-tions, or in support of opinions; but is it not somewhat unreasonable vehemently to condemn a writer for not exhausting himself, and his readers, by discussing pleas which are not only unsound in themselves, but irrele-vant to the direct purpose of his work? I have only advanced objections against the Johannine authorship of the fourth Gospel, which seem to me unrefuted by any of the explanations offered.

Let me now turn to more important instances. Dr. Lightfoot asks: "Why, when he is endeavouring to minimise, if not deny, the Hebraic character of the fourth Gospel, does he wholly ignore the investigations of Luthardt and others, which (as 'apologists' venture to think) show that the whole texture of the language in the fourth Gospel is Hebraic?" [2] Now my state-ments with regard to the language of the Apocalypse and fourth Gospel are as follows. Of the Apocalypse I say: "The language in which the book is written is the

[1] *Contemporary Review*, p. 11 f. [*ibid.* p. 16].   [2] *Ibid.* p. 10 [*ibid.* p. 14].

most Hebraistic Greek of the New Testament;"[1] and further on: "The barbarous Hebraistic Greek and abrupt, inelegant diction are natural to the unlettered fisherman of Galilee."[2] Of the Gospel I say: "Instead of the Hebraistic Greek and harsh diction which might be expected from the unlettered and ignorant[3] fisherman of Galilee, we find, in the fourth Gospel, the purest and least Hebraistic Greek of any of the Gospels (some parts of the third synoptic, perhaps, alone excepted), and a refinement and beauty of composition whose charm has captivated the world," &c.[4] In another place I say: "The language in which the Gospel is written, as we have already mentioned, is much less Hebraic than that of the other Gospels, with the exception, perhaps, of parts of the Gospel according to Luke, and its Hebraisms are not on the whole greater than was almost invariably the case with Hellenistic Greek; but its composition is distinguished by peculiar smoothness, grace, and beauty, and in this respect it is assigned the first rank amongst the Gospels."[5] I believe that I do not say another word as to the texture of the language of the fourth Gospel, and it will be observed that my remarks are almost wholly limited to the comparative quality of the Greek of the fourth Gospel, on the one hand, and the Apocalypse and Synoptics on the other, and that they do not exclude Hebraisms. The views expressed might be supported by numberless authorities. As Dr. Lightfoot accuses me of "wholly ignoring" the results at which Luthardt and others have arrived, I will quote what Luthardt says of the two works: "The difference of the *language*, as well in regard to grammar and style as to doctrine, is, of course, in a high degree remarkable. . . . As regards *grammar*, the Gospel is

[1] *S. R.* ii. p. 402.   [2] *Ibid.* ii. p. 406.
[3] See Acts iv. 13.   [4] *S. R.* ii. p. 410.   [5] *Ibid.* ii. p. 413.

written in correct, the Apocalypse in incorrect Greek."
He argues that this is a consequence of sovereign freedom in the latter, and that from the nature of the
composition the author of the Apocalypse wrote in an
artificial style, and could both have spoken and written
otherwise. "The errors are not errors of ignorance,
but intentional emancipations from the rules of grammar" (!), in imitation of ancient prophetic style. Presently he proceeds: "If, then, on the one hand, the
Apocalypse is written in worse Greek and less correctly
than its author was able to speak and write, the question, on the other hand, is, whether the Gospel is not
in too good Greek to be credited to a born Jew and
Palestinian." Luthardt maintains "that the style of the
Gospel betrays the born Jew, and certainly not the
Greek," but the force which he intends to give to all
this reasoning is clearly indicated by the conclusion at
which he finally arrives, that "the linguistic gulf between
the Gospel and the Apocalypse is not impassable." [1]
This result from so staunch an apologist, obviously
seeking to minimise the Hebraic character of the Apocalypse, is not after all so strikingly different from my
representation. Take again the opinion of so eminent
an apologist as Bleek: "The language of the Apocalypse
in its whole character is beyond comparison harsher,
rougher, looser, and presents grosser incorrectness than
any other book of the New Testament, whilst the language of the Gospel is certainly not pure Greek, but is
beyond comparison more grammatically correct." [2] I am
merely replying to the statements of Dr. Lightfoot, and
not arguing afresh regarding the language of the fourth
Gospel, or I might produce very different arguments
and authorities, but I may remark that the critical

---

[1] *Der Johann. Ursp. des viert. Evang.* 1874, pp. 204–7.
[2] *Einl. N. T.* p. 625.

dilemma which I have represented, in reviewing the fourth Gospel, is not merely dependent upon linguistic considerations, but arises out of the aggregate and con- flicting phenomena presented by the Apocalypse on the one hand and the Gospel on the other.

Space only allows of my referring to one other instance.[1]   Dr. Lightfoot says—

"If by any chance he condescends to discuss a question, he takes care to fasten on the least likely solution of 'apologists' (e.g. the identification of Sychar and Shechem),[2] omitting altogether to notice others."

In a note Dr. Lightfoot adds—

"Travellers and 'apologists' alike now more commonly identify Sychar with the village bearing the Arabic name Askar.   This fact is not mentioned by our author.   He says moreover, 'It is ad- mitted that there was no such place (as Sychar, Συχάρ), and apologetic ingenuity is severely taxed to explain the difficulty.' *This is altogether untrue.*   Others besides 'apologists' point to passages in the Talmud which speak of 'the well of Suchar (or Sochar or Sichar);' see Neubauer, 'La Géographie du Talmud,' p. 169 f.   Our author refers in his note to an article by Delitzsch, 'Zeitschr. J. Luth. Theol.,' 1856, p. 240 f.)   *He cannot have read the article, for these Talmudic references are its main purport."*[3]

I may perhaps be allowed to refer, first, to the two sentences which I have taken the liberty of putting in italics.   If it be possible for an apologist to apologise, an apology is surely due to the readers of the "Con- temporary Review," at least, for this style of criticism, to which, I doubt not, they are as little accustomed as I am myself.   There is no satisfying Dr. Lightfoot.   I give him references, and he accuses me of "literary

---

[1] In regard to one other point, I may say that, so far from being silent about the presence of a form of the Logos doctrine in the Apocalypse with which Dr. Lightfoot reproaches me, I repeatedly point out its existence, as, for instance, *S. R.* ii. pp. 255, 273, 278, &c., and I also show its presence elsewhere, my argument being that the doctrine not only was not originated by the fourth Gospel, but that it had already been applied to Christianity in N. T. writings before the composition of that work.

[2] *S. R.* ii. 421.   [3] *Contemporary Review,* 12 f. [*ibid.* p. 17 f.]

browbeating" and " subtle intimidation ; " I do not give references, and he gives me the lie. I refer to the article of Delitzsch in support of my specific statement that he rejects the identification of Sychar with Sichem, and apparently because I do not quote the whole study Dr. Lightfoot courteously asserts that I cannot have read it.[1]

My statement [2] is, that it is admitted that there was no such place as Sychar—I ought to have added, " except by apologists who never admit anything "—but I thought that in saying : " and apologetic ingenuity is severely taxed to explain the difficulty," I had sufficiently excepted apologists, and indicated that many assertions and conjectures are advanced by them for that purpose. I mention that the conjecture which identifies Sychar and Sichem is rejected by some, refer to Credner's supposition that the alteration may be due to some error committed by a secretary in writing down the Gospel from the dictation of the Apostle, and that Sichem is meant, and I state the " nickname " hypothesis of Hengstenberg and others. It is undeniable that, with the exception of some vague references in the Talmud to a somewhat similar, but not identical, name, the locality of which is quite uncertain, no place bearing, or having borne, the designation of Sychar is known. The ordinary apologetic theory, as Dr. Lightfoot may find "in any common source of information,"—Dr. Smith's " Dictionary of the Bible," for instance—is the delightfully comprehensive one : " Sychar was either a name applied to the town of Shechem, or it was an independent place." This authority, however, goes clean against Dr. Lightfoot's assertion, for it continues : " The first of these

[1] Dr. Lightfoot will find the passage to which I refer, more especially p. 241, line 4, commencing with the words, "Nur zwei neuere Ausleger ahnen die einfache Wahrheit."

[2] *S. R.* 421 f.

alternatives is now almost universally accepted." Light-foot [1] considered Sychar a mere alteration of the name Sichem, both representing the same place.   He found a reference in the Talmud to "*Ain Socar,*" and with great hesitation he associated the name with Sychar.   "May we not venture" to render it "the well of Sychar"? And after detailed extracts and explanations he says: "And now let the reader give us his judgment as to its name and place, whether it doth not seem to have some rela-tion with our 'well of Sychar.' It may be disputed on either side."   Wieseler, who first, in more recent times, developed the conjectures of Lightfoot, argues: "In the first place, there can be no doubt that by Συχάρ Sichem is meant," and he adds, a few lines after: "Regarding this there is no controversy amongst interpreters."   He totally rejects the idea of such an alteration of the name occurring in translation, which he says is "unprece-dented." He therefore concludes that in Συχάρ we have *another* name for Sichem.   He merely submits this, however, as "a new hypothesis to the judgment of the reader," [2] which alone shows the uncertainty of the suggestion.   Lightfoot and Wieseler are substantially followed by Olshausen, [3] De Wette, [4] Hug, [5] Bunsen, [6] Rig-genbach, [7] Godet, [8] and others.   Bleek, [9] in spite of the arguments of Delitzsch and Ewald, and their Talmudic researches, considers that the old town of Sichem is meant.   Delitzsch, [10] Ewald, [11] Lange, [12] Meyer, [13] and others

---

[1] *Works*, ed. Pitman, x. 339 f.; *Horæ Hebræ et Talm.* p. 938.

[2] *Chron. Synopse d. vier. Evv.* p. 256, Anm. 1.

[3] *Bibl. Comm., Das. Ev. n. Joh.,* umgearb. Ebrard ii. 1, p. 122 f.

[4] *Kurzgef. ex. Handbuch N. T.* i. 3, p. 84.

[5] *Einl. N. T.* ii. 194 f. Hug more strictly applies the name to the sepulchre where the bones of Joseph were laid (Josh. xxiv. 32).

[6] *Bibelwerk,* iv. 210.   [7] *Die Zeugnisse, u.s.w.* p. 21.

[8] *Comm. sur l'Ev. de St. Jean,* i. p. 475 f.   [9] *Einl. N. T.* p. 211.

[10] *Zeitschr. gesammt. Luth. Theol. u. Kirche,* 1856, p. 240 ff.

[11] *Die Joh. Schriften,* i. p. 181, Anm. 1 ; *Jahrb. bibl. Wiss.* viii. p. 255 f. ; cf. *Gesch. v. Isr.* v. p. 348, Anm. 1.

[12] *Das Ev. Joh.* p. 107.   [13] *Comm. Ev. n. Joh.* p. 188 f.

think that Sychar was near to, but distinct from, Sichem. Lücke[1] is very undecided. He recognises the extraordinary difference in the name Sychar. He does not favourably receive Lightfoot's arguments regarding an alteration of the name of Sichem, nor his conjectures as to the relation of the place mentioned in the Talmud to Sichem, which he thinks is "very doubtful," and he seems to incline rather to an accidental corruption of Sichem into Sychar, although he feels the great difficulties in the way of such an explanation. Ewald condemns the "Talmudische Studien" of Delitzsch as generally more complicating than clearing up difficulties, and his views as commonly incorrect, and, whilst agreeing with him that Sychar cannot be the same place as Sichem, he points out that the site of the *valley of the well* of the Talmud is certainly doubtful.[2] He explains his own views, however, more clearly in another place :—

"That this (Sychar) cannot be the large, ancient Sikhem, which, at the time when the Gospel was written, was probably already generally called *Neapolis* in Greek writings, has been already stated ; it is the place still called with an altered Arabic name *Al 'Askar*, east of Naplûs. It is indeed difficult to prove that Sychar could stand for Sikhem, either through change of pronunciation, or for any other reason, and the addition λεγομένη does not indicate, here any more than in xi. 54, so large and generally known a town as Sikhem or Flavia Neapolis."[3]

Mr. Sanday,[4] of whose able work Dr. Lightfoot directly speaks, says :—

"The name Sychar is not the common one, Sichem, but is a mock title (='liar' or 'drunkard') that was given to the town by the Jews.[5] This is a clear reminiscence of the vernacular that the

[1] *Comm. Ev. des Joh.* i. p. 577 f.   [2] *Jahrb. bibl. Wiss.* viii. p. 255 f.
[3] *Die Joh. Schr.* i. p. 181, Anm. 1.
[4] *Authorship and Hist. Char. of Fourth Gospel*, 1872, p. 92.
[5] Mr. Sanday adds in a note here: "This may perhaps be called the current explanation of the name. It is accepted as well by those who deny

Apostle spoke in his youth, and is a strong touch of nature. It is not quite certain that the name Sychar has this force, but the hypothesis is in itself more likely than, &c. . . . It is not, however, by any means improbable that Sychar may represent, not Sichem, but the modern village Askar, which is somewhat nearer to Jacob's Well."

To quote one of the latest "travellers and apologists," Dr. Farrar says: "From what the name Sychar is derived is uncertain. The word λεγόμενος in St. John seems to imply a sobriquet. It may be 'a lie,' 'drunken,' or 'a sepulchre.' Sychar may possibly have been a village nearer the well than Sichem, on the site of the village now called El Askar."[1] As Dr. Lightfoot specially mentions Neubauer, his opinion may be substantially given in a single sentence: "La Mischna mentionne un endroit appelé 'la plaine d'En-Sokher,' qui est peut-être le Sychar de l'Evangile." He had a few lines before said: "Il est donc plus logique de ne pas identifier Sychar avec Sichem."[2] Now, with regard to all these theories, and especially in so far as they connect Sychar with El Askar, let me quote a few more words in conclusion, from a "common source of information:"—

"On the other hand there is an etymological difficulty in the way of this identification. 'Askar begins with the letter 'Ain, which Sychar does not appear to have contained ; a letter too stubborn and enduring to be easily either dropped or assumed in a name. . . . These considerations have been stated not so much with the hope of leading to any conclusion on the identity of Sychar, which seems hopeless, as with the desire to show that the ordinary explanation is not nearly so obvious as it is usually assumed to be."[3]

Mr. Grove is very right.

I have been careful only to quote from writers who

the genuineness of the Gospel as by those who maintain it. Cf. Keim, i. 133.   But there is much to be said for the identification with El Askar, &c." *Authorship and Hist. Char. of Fourth Gospel*, p. 93, note 1.
    [1] *Life of Christ*, i. p. 206, note 1.   [2] *La Géographie du Talmud*, p. 170.
    [3] Smith's *Dictionary of the Bible*, iii. p. 1305 f.

are either "apologetic," or far from belonging to hetero-
dox schools. Is it not perfectly clear that no place of
the name of Sychar can be reasonably identified? The
case, in fact, simply stands thus :—As the Gospel mentions a town called Sychar, apologists maintain that
there must have been such a place, and attempt by
various theories to find a site for it. It is certain,
however, that even in the days of St. Jerome there
was no real trace of such a town, and apologists and
travellers have not since been able to discover it, except
in their own imaginations.

With regard to the insinuation that the references
given in my notes constitute a "subtle mode of intimidation" and "literary browbeating," Canon Lightfoot
omits to say that I as fully and candidly refer to those
who maintain views wholly different from my own, as
to those who support me. It is very possible, considering the number of these references, that I may have
committed some errors, and I can only say that I shall
very thankfully receive from Dr. Lightfoot any correc-
tions which he may be good enough to point out.
Instead of intimidation and browbeating, my sole desire
has been to indicate to all who may be anxious further
to examine questions in debate, works in which they
may find them discussed. It is time that the system of
advancing apologetic opinions with perfect assurance,
and without a hint that they are disputed by anyone,
should come to an end, and that earnest men should be
made acquainted with the true state of the case. As
Dr. Mozley rightly and honestly says : "The majority
of mankind, perhaps, owe their belief rather to the out-
ward influence of custom and education than to any
strong principle of faith within ; and it is to be feared
that many, if they came to perceive how wonderful what
they believed was, would not find their belief so easy

and so matter-of-course a thing as they appear to find
it." [1]

I shall not here follow Dr. Lightfoot into his general
remarks regarding my 'conclusions,' nor shall I proceed, in this article, to discuss the dilemma in which he
attempts to involve me through his misunderstanding
and consequent misstatement, of my views regarding
the Supreme Being. I am almost inclined to think that
I can have the pleasure of agreeing with him in one important point, at least, before coming to a close. When
I read the curiously modified statement that I have
" studiously avoided committing myself to a belief in a
universal Father, or a moral Governor, or even in a
Personal God," it seems clear to me that the *Supernatural Religion* about which Dr. Lightfoot has been
writing cannot be my work, but is simply a work of
his own imagination. That work cannot possibly have
contained, for instance, the chapter on " Anthropomorphic Divinity," [2] in which, on the contrary, I studiously
commit myself to very decided disbelief in such a "Personal God " as he means. In no way inconsistent with
that chapter are my concluding remarks, contrasting
with the spasmodic Jewish Divinity a Supreme Being
manifested in the operation of invariable laws—whose
very invariability is the guarantee of beneficence and
security. If Dr. Lightfoot, however, succeeded in con-
victing me of inconsistency in those final expressions,
there could be no doubt which view must logically be
abandoned, and it would be a new sensation to secure
the approval of a divine by the unhesitating destruction
of the last page of my work.

Dr. Lightfoot, again, refers to Mr. Mill's "Three
Essays on Religion," but he does not appear to have
very deeply studied that work. I confess that I do not

---

[1] *Bampton Lect.* 1865, 2nd edit. p. 4.   [2] *S. R.* i. p. 61 ff.

entirely agree with some views therein expressed, and I hope that, hereafter, I may have an opportunity of explaining what they are; but I am surprised that Dr. Lightfoot has failed to observe how singularly that great Thinker supports the general results of *Supernatural Religion*, to the point even of a frequent agreement almost in words. If Dr. Lightfoot had studied Mill a little more closely, he would not have committed the serious error of arguing: "Obviously, if the author has established his conclusions in the first part, the second and third are altogether superfluous. It is somewhat strange, therefore, that more than three-fourths of the whole work should be devoted to this needless task."[1] Now my argument in the first part is not that miracles are impossible—a thesis which it is quite unnecessary to maintain—but the much more simple one that miracles are *antecedently* incredible. Having shown that they are so, and appreciated the true nature of the allegation of miracles, and the amount of evidence requisite to establish it, I proceed to examine the evidence which is actually produced in support of the assertion that, although miracles are antecedently incredible, they nevertheless took place. Mr. Mill clearly supports me in this course. He states the main principle of my argument thus: "A revelation, therefore, cannot be proved divine unless ·by external evidence; that is, by the exhibition of supernatural facts. And we have to consider, whether it is possible to prove supernatural facts, and if it is, what evidence is required to prove them."[2] Mr. Mill decides that it is possible to prove the occurrence of a supernatural fact, if it actually occurred, and after showing the great preponderance of evidence against miracles, he says: "Against this

---

[1] *Contemporary Review*, p. 19 [*ibid.* p. 26 f.]
[2] *Three Essays on Religion*, p. 216 f.

weight of negative evidence we have to set such positive evidence as is produced in attestation of exceptions; in other words, the positive evidences of miracles. And I have already admitted that this evidence might conceivably have been such as to make the exception equally certain with the rule." [1] Mr. Mill's opinion of the evidence actually produced is not flattering, and may be compared with my results :—

"But the evidence of miracles, at least to Protestant Christians, is not, in our day, of this cogent description. It is not the evidence of our senses, but of witnesses, and even this not at first hand, but resting on the attestation of books and traditions. And even in the case of the original eye-witnesses, the supernatural facts asserted on their alleged testimony are not of the transcendent character supposed in our example, about the nature of which, or the impossibility of their having had a natural origin, there could be little room for doubt. On the contrary, the recorded miracles are, in the first place, generally such as it would have been extremely difficult to verify as matters of fact, and in the next place, are hardly ever beyond the possibility of having been brought about by human means or by the spontaneous agencies of nature." [2]

It is to substantiate the statements made here, and, in fact, to confirm the philosophical conclusion by the historical proof, that I enter into an examination of the four Gospels, as the chief witnesses for miracles. To those who have already ascertained the frivolous nature of that testimony it may, no doubt, seem useless labour to examine it in detail; but it is scarcely conceivable that an ecclesiastic who professes to base his faith upon those records should represent such a process as useless. In endeavouring to place me on the forks of a dilemma, in fact, Dr. Lightfoot has betrayed that he altogether fails to appreciate the question at issue, or to comprehend the position of miracles in relation to philosophical and historical enquiry. Instead of being "altogether

[1] *Three Essays on Religion*, p. 234.   [2] *Ibid.* p. 210.

superfluous," my examination of witnesses, in the second and third parts, has more correctly been represented by able critics as incomplete, from the omission of the remaining documents of the New Testament. I foresaw, and myself to some degree admitted, the justice of this argument;[1] but my work being already bulky enough, I reserved to another volume the completion of the enquiry.

I cannot close this article without expressing my regret that so much which is personal and unworthy has been introduced into the discussion of a great and profoundly important subject. Dr. Lightfoot is too able and too earnest a man not to recognise that no occasional errors or faults in a writer can really affect the validity of his argument, and instead of mere general and desultory efforts to do some damage to me, it would be much more to the purpose were he seriously to endeavour to refute my reasoning. I have no desire to escape hard hitting or to avoid fair fight, and I feel unfeigned respect for many of my critics who, differing *toto cœlo* from my views, have with vigorous ability attacked my arguments without altogether forgetting the courtesy due even to an enemy. Dr. Lightfoot will not find me inattentive to courteous reasoning, nor indifferent to earnest criticism, and, whatever he may think, I promise him that no one will be more ready respectfully to follow every serious line of argument than the author of *Supernatural Religion.*

---

[1] *S. R.* ii, p. 477.

II.

THE SILENCE OF EUSEBIUS—THE IGNATIAN EPISTLES.[1]

THIS work has scarcely yet been twelve months before the public, but both in this country and in America and elsewhere it has been subjected to such wide and searching criticism by writers of all shades of opinion, that I may perhaps be permitted to make a few remarks, and to review some of my Reviewers. I must first, however, beg leave to express my gratitude to that large majority of my critics who have bestowed generous commendation upon the work, and liberally encouraged its completion. I have to thank others, who, differing totally from my conclusions, have nevertheless temperately argued against them, for the courtesy with which they have treated an opponent whose views must necessarily have offended them, and I can only say that, whilst such a course has commanded my unfeigned respect, it has certainly not diminished the attention with which I have followed their arguments.

There are two serious misapprehensions of the purpose and line of argument of this work which I desire to correct. Some critics have objected that, if I had succeeded in establishing the proposition advanced in the first part, the second and third parts need not have

---

[1] This appeared as the Preface to the 6th edition.

been written: in fact, that the historical argument against miracles is only necessary in consequence of the failure of the philosophical. Now I contend that the historical is the necessary complement of the philosophical argument, and that both are equally requisite to completeness in dealing with the subject. The preliminary affirmation is not that miracles are impossible, but that they are antecedently incredible. The counter-allegation is that, although miracles may be antecedently incredible, they nevertheless actually took place. It is, therefore, necessary, not only to establish the antecedent incredibility, but to examine the validity of the allegation that certain miracles occurred, and this involves the historical enquiry into the evidence for the Gospels which occupies the second and third parts. Indeed, many will not acknowledge the case to be complete until other witnesses are questioned in a succeeding volume. . . .

The second point to which I desire to refer is a statement which has frequently been made that, in the second and third parts, I endeavour to prove that the four canonical Gospels were not written until the end of the second century. This error is of course closely connected with that which has just been discussed, but it is difficult to understand how anyone who had taken the slightest trouble to ascertain the nature of the argument, and to state it fairly, could have fallen into it. The fact is that no attempt is made to prove anything with regard to the Gospels. The evidence for them is merely examined, and it is found that, so far from their affording sufficient testimony to warrant belief in the actual occurrence of miracles declared to be antecedently incredible, there is not a certain trace even of the existence of the Gospels for a century and a half after those miracles are alleged to have occurred, and nothing whatever to attest their authenticity and truth. This is a very different thing from an endeavour to establish some special theory of my own, and it is because this line of argument has not been understood, that some critics have expressed surprise at the decisive rejection of mere conjectures and possibilities as evidence. In a case of such importance, no testimony which is not clear and indubitable could be of any value, but the evidence producible for the canonical Gospels falls very far short even of ordinary requirements, and in relation to miracles it is scarcely deserving of serious consideration.

It has been argued that, even if there be no evidence for our special gospels, I admit that gospels very similar must early have been in existence, and that these equally represent the same prevailing belief as the canonical Gospels: consequently that I merely change, without shaking, the witnesses. Those who advance this argument, however, totally overlook the fact that it is not the reality of the superstitious belief which is in question, but the reality of the miracles, and the sufficiency of the witnesses to establish them. What such objectors urge practically amounts to this: that we should believe in the actual occurrence of certain miracles contradictory to all experience, out of a mass of false miracles which are reported but never really took place, because some unknown persons in an ignorant and superstitious age, who give no evidence of personal knowledge, or of careful investigation, have written an account of them, and other persons, equally ignorant and superstitious, have believed them. I venture to say that no one who advances the argument to which I am referring can have realised the nature of the question at issue, and the relation of miracles to the order of nature.

The last of these general objections to which I need now refer is the statement, that the difficulty with regard to the Gospels commences precisely where my examination ends, and that I am bound to explain how, if no trace of their existence is previously discoverable, the four Gospels are suddenly found in general circulation at the end of the second century, and quoted as authoritative documents by such writers as Irenæus. My reply is that it is totally unnecessary for me to account for this. No one acquainted with the history of pseudonymic literature in the second century, and with the rapid circulation and ready acceptance of spurious works tending to edification, could for a moment regard the canonical position of any Gospel at the end of that century either as evidence of its authenticity or early origin. That which concerns us chiefly is not evidence regarding the end of the second but the beginning of the first century. Even if we took the statements of Irenæus and later Fathers, like the Alexandrian Clement, Tertullian and Origen, about the Gospels, they are absolutely without value except as personal opinion at a late date, for which no sufficient grounds are shown. Of the earlier history of those Gospels there is not a distinct trace, except of a nature which altogether discredits them as witnesses for miracles.

After having carefully weighed the arguments which have been advanced against this work, I venture to express strengthened conviction of the truth of its conclusions. The best and most powerful reasons which able divines and apologists have been able to bring forward against its main argument have, I submit, not only failed to shake it, but have, by inference, shown it to be unassailable. Very many of those who have professedly advanced against the citadel itself have practically attacked nothing but some outlying fort, which was scarcely worth defence, whilst others, who have seriously attempted an assault, have shown that the Church has no artillery capable of making a practicable breach in the rationalistic stronghold. I say this solely in reference to the argument which I have taken upon myself to represent, and in no sense of my own individual share in its maintenance.

I must now address myself more particularly to two of my critics who, with great ability and learning, have subjected this work to the most elaborate and microscopic criticism of which personal earnestness and official zeal are capable. I am sincerely obliged to Professor Lightfoot and Dr. Westcott for the minute attention they have bestowed upon my book. I had myself directly attacked the views of Dr. Westcott, and of course could only expect him to do his best or his worst against me in reply; and I am not surprised at the vigour with which Dr. Lightfoot has assailed a work so opposed to principles which he himself holds sacred, although I may be permitted to express my regret that he has not done so in a spirit more worthy of the cause which he defends. In spite of hostile criticism of very unusual minuteness and ability, no flaw or error has been pointed out which in the slightest degree affects my main argument, and I consider that every point yet objected to by Dr. Lightfoot, or indicated by Dr. Westcott, might be withdrawn without at all weakening my position. These objections, I may say, refer solely to details, and only follow side issues, but the attack, if impotent against the main position, has in many cases been insidiously directed against notes and passing references, and a plentiful sprinkling of such words as "misstatements" and "misrepresentations" along the line may have given it a formidable appearance and malicious effect, which render it worth while once for all to meet it in detail.

The first point to which I shall refer is an elaborate argument by Dr. Lightfoot regarding the " SILENCE OF EUSEBIUS." [1] I had called attention to the importance of considering the silence of the Fathers, under certain conditions; [2] and I might, omitting his curious limitation, adopt Dr. Lightfoot's opening comment upon this as singularly descriptive of the state of the case : " In one province more especially, relating to the external evidences for the Gospels, silence occupies a prominent place." Dr. Lightfoot proposes to interrogate this " mysterious oracle," and he considers that " the response elicited will not be at all ambiguous." I might again agree with him, but that unambiguous response can scarcely be pronounced very satisfactory for the Gospels. Such silence may be very eloquent, but after all it is only the eloquence of—silence. I have not yet met with the argument anywhere that, because none of the early Fathers quote our Canonical Gospels, or say anything with regard to them, the fact is unambiguous evidence that they were well acquainted with them, and considered them apostolic and authoritative. Dr. Lightfoot's argument from Silence is, for the present at least, limited to Eusebius.

The point on which the argument turns is this: After examining the whole of the extant writings of the early Fathers, and finding them a complete blank as regards the canonical Gospels, if, by their use of apocryphal works and other indications, they are not evidence against them, I supplement this, in the case of Hegesippus, Papias, and Dionysius of Corinth, by the inference that, as Eusebius does not state that their lost

---

[1] *Contemporary Review*, January 1875, p. 1 ff. (*Ibid.* p. 32 ff.)
[2] *S. R.* i. p. 212.

works contained any evidence for the Gospels, they actually did not contain any. But before proceeding to discuss the point, it is necessary that a proper estimate should be formed of its importance to the main argument of my work. The evident labour which Professor Lightfoot has expended upon the preparation of his attack, the space devoted to it, and his own express words, would naturally lead most readers to suppose that it has almost a vital bearing upon my conclusions. Dr. Lightfoot says, after quoting the passages in which I appeal to the silence of Eusebius :—

"This indeed is the fundamental assumption which lies at the basis of his reasoning ; and the reader will not need to be reminded how much of the argument falls to pieces if this basis should prove to be unsound. A wise master-builder would therefore have looked to his foundations first, and assured himself of their strength, before he piled up his fabric to this height. This our author has altogether neglected to do." [1]

Towards the close of his article, after triumphantly expressing his belief that his " main conclusions are irrefragable," he further says :—

"If they are, then the reader will not fail to see how large a part of the argument in *Supernatural Religion* has crumbled to pieces." [2]

I do not doubt that Dr. Lightfoot sincerely believes this, but he must allow me to say that he is thoroughly mistaken in his estimate of the importance of the point, and that, as regards this work, the representations made in the above passages are a very strange exaggeration. I am unfortunately too familiar, in connection with criticism on this book, with instances of vast expenditure of time and strength in attacking points to which I attach no importance whatever, and which in themselves have scarcely any value. When writers, after an

[1] *Contemporary Review*, January 1875, p. 172 [*ibid.* p. 30].
[2] *Ibid.* p. 183 [*ibid.* p. 51].

amount of demonstration which must have conveyed
the impression that vital interests were at stake, have,
at least in their own opinion, proved that I have omitted
to dot an " i," cross a " t," or insert an inverted comma,
they have really left the question precisely where it was.
Now, in the present instance, the whole extent of the
argument which is based upon the silence of Eusebius
is an inference regarding some lost works of three
writers only, which might altogether be withdrawn
without affecting the case. The object of my investigation is to discover what evidence actually exists in the
works of early writers regarding our Gospels. In the
fragments which remain of the works of three writers,
Hegesippus, Papias, and Dionysius of Corinth, I do not
find any evidence of acquaintance with these Gospels,—
the works mentioned by Papias being, I contend, different from the existing Gospels attributed to Matthew
and Mark. Whether I am right or not in this does not
affect the present discussion. It is an unquestioned
fact that Eusebius does not mention that the lost works
of these writers contained any reference to, or information about, the Gospels, nor have we any statement
from any other author to that effect. The objection of
Dr. Lightfoot is limited to a denial that the silence of
Eusebius warrants the inference that, because he does
not state that these writers made quotations from or
references to undisputed canonical books, the lost
works did not contain any ; it does not, however, extend to interesting information regarding those books,
which he admits it was the purpose of Eusebius to
record. To give Dr. Lightfoot's statements, which I
am examining, the fullest possible support, however,
suppose that I abandon Eusebius altogether, and do
not draw any inference of any kind from him beyond
his positive statements, how would my case stand ?

Simply as complete as it well could be : Hegesippus, Papias, and Dionysius do not furnish any evidence in favour of the Gospels. The reader, therefore, will not fail to see how serious a misstatement Dr. Lightfoot has made, and how little the argument of *Supernatural Religion* would be affected even if he established much more than he has asserted.

We may now proceed to consider Dr. Lightfoot's argument itself. He carefully and distinctly defines what he understands to be the declared intention of Eusebius in composing his history, as regards the mention or use of the disputed and undisputed canonical books in the writings of the Fathers, and in order to do him full justice I will quote his words, merely taking the liberty, for facility of reference, of dividing his statement into three paragraphs. He says :—

"Eusebius therefore proposes to treat these two classes of writings in two different ways. This is the cardinal point of the passage.

"(1) Of the Antilegomena he pledges himself to record when any ancient writer *employs* any book belonging to their class (τίνες ὁποίαις κέχρηνται) ;

"(2) but as regards the undisputed Canonical books, he only professes to mention them when such a writer has something to *tell about them* (τίνα περὶ τῶν ἐνδιαθήκων εἴρηται). Any *anecdote* of interest respecting them, as also respecting the others (τῶν μὴ τοιούτων), will be recorded.

"(3) But in their case he nowhere leads us to expect that he will allude to mere *quotations*, however numerous and however precise."[1]

In order to dispose of the only one of these points upon which we can differ, I will first refer to the third. Did Eusebius intend to point out mere quotations of the books which he considered undisputed? As a matter of fact, he actually did point such out in the case of the 1st Epistle of Peter and the 1st Epistle of John, which he repeatedly and in the most emphatic

---

[1] *Contemporary Review*, January 1875, p. 173 [*ibid.* p. 38].

manner declared to be undisputed.[1] This is admitted by Dr. Lightfoot. That he omitted to mention a reference to the Epistle to the Corinthians in the Epistle of Clement of Rome, or the reference by Theophilus to the Gospel of John, and other supposed quotations, might be set down as much to oversight as intention. On the other hand, that he did mention disputed books is evidence only that he not only pledged himself to do so, but actually fulfilled his promise. Although much might be said upon this point, therefore, I consider it of so little importance that I do not intend to waste time in minutely discussing it. If my assertions with regard to the silence of Eusebius likewise include the supposition that he proposed to mention mere quotations of the "undisputed" books, they are so far from limited to this very subsidiary testimony that I should have no reluctance in waiving it altogether. Even if the most distinct quotations of this kind had occurred in the lost works of the three writers in question, they could have proved nothing beyond the mere existence of the book quoted, at the time that work was written, but would have done nothing to establish its authenticity and trustworthiness. In the evidential destitution of the Gospels, apologists would thankfully have received even such vague indications; indeed there is scarcely any other evidence, but something much more definite is required to establish the reality of miracles and Divine Revelation. If this point be, for the sake of argument, set aside, what is the position? We are not entitled to infer that there were no quotations from the Gospels in the works of Hegesippus, Papias, and Diony-

---

[1] I regret very much that some ambiguity in my language (*S. R.* i. p. 483) should have misled, and given Dr. Lightfoot much trouble. I used the word "quotation" in the sense of a use of the Epistle of Peter, and not in reference to any one sentence in Polycarp. I trust that in this edition I have made my meaning clear.

sius of Corinth, because Eusebius does not record them ; but, on the other hand, we are still less entitled to infer that there were any.

The only inference which I care to draw from the silence of Eusebius is precisely that which Dr. Lightfoot admits that, both from his promise and practice, I am entitled to deduce : when any ancient writer "has something to *tell about*" the Gospels, "any *anecdote* of interest respecting them," Eusebius will record it. This is the only information of the slightest value to this work which could be looked for in these writers. So far, therefore, from producing the destructive effect upon some of the arguments of *Supernatural Religion*, upon which he somewhat prematurely congratulates himself, Dr. Lightfoot's elaborate and learned article on the silence of Eusebius supports them in the most conclusive manner.

Before proceeding to speak more directly of the three writers under discussion, it may be well to glance a little at the procedure of Eusebius, and note, for those who care to go more closely into the matter, how he fulfils his promise to record what the Fathers have to tell about the Gospels. I may mention, in the first place, that Eusebius states what he himself knows of the composition of the Gospels and other canonical works.[1] Upon two occasions he quotes the account which Clement of Alexandria gives of the composition of Mark's Gospel, and also cites his statements regarding the other Gospels.[2] In like manner he records the information, such as it is, which Irenæus has to impart about the four Gospels and other works,[3] and what Origen has to say concerning them.[4] Interrogating extant works, we find in fact that Eusebius does not neglect to quote anything useful or interesting regarding these books from early writers. Dr. Lightfoot says that Eusebius " restricts himself to the narrowest limits which justice to his subject will allow," and he illustrates this by the case of Irenæus. He says : " Though he (Eusebius) gives the principal passage in this author

---

[1] Cf. *H. E.* iii. 3, 4, 18, 24, 25, &c. &c.   [2] *Ibid.* ii. 15, vi. 14.
[3] *Ibid.* v. 8.   [4] *Ibid.* vi. 25.

relating to the Four Gospels (Irenæus, *Adv. Hær.* iii. 1, 1) he omits to mention others which contain interesting statements directly or indirectly affecting the question, *e.g.* that St. John wrote his Gospel to counteract the errors of Cerinthus and the Nicolaitans (Irenæus, *Adv. Hær.* iii. 11, 1)."[1] I must explain, however, that the "interesting statement" omitted, which is not in the context of the part quoted, is not advanced as information derived from any authority, but only in the course of argument, and there is nothing to distinguish it from mere personal opinion, so that on this ground Eusebius may well have passed it over. Dr. Lightfoot further says : "Thus too when he quotes a few lines alluding to the unanimous tradition of the Asiatic Elders who were acquainted with St. John,[2] he omits the context, from which we find that this tradition had an important bearing on the authenticity of the fourth Gospel, for it declared that Christ's ministry extended much beyond a single year, thus confirming the obvious chronology of the Fourth Gospel against the apparent chronology of the Synoptists."[3] Nothing, however, could be further from the desire or intention of Eusebius than to represent any discordance between the Gospels, or to support the one at the expense of the others. On the contrary, he enters into an elaborate explanation in order to show that there is no discrepancy between them, affirming, and supporting his view by singular quotations, that it was evidently the intention of the three Synoptists only to write the doings of the Lord for one year after the imprisonment of John the Baptist, and that John, having the other Gospels before him, wrote an account of the period not embraced by the other evangelists.[4] Moreover, the extraordinary assertions of Irenæus not only contradict the Synoptics, but also the Fourth Gospel, and Eusebius certainly could not have felt much inclination to quote such opinions, even although Irenæus seemed to base them upon traditions handed down by the Presbyters who were acquainted with John.

It being, then, admitted that Eusebius not only pledges himself to record when any ancient writer has something to "tell about" the undisputed canonical books, but that, judged by the test of extant writings

---

[1] *Contemporary Review*, January 1875, p. 181 [*ibid. p.* 48].
[2] By a slip of the pen Dr. Lightfoot refers to Irenæus, *Adv. Hær.* iii. 3, 4. It should be ii. 22, 5.
[3] *Ibid.* p. 181. [4] *H. E.* iii. 24.

which we can examine, he actually does so, let us
see the conclusions which we are entitled to draw in
the case of the only three writers with regard to
whom I have inferred anything from the "silence of
Eusebius."

I need scarcely repeat that Eusebius held HEGESIP-
PUS in very high estimation. He refers to him very
frequently, and he clearly shows that he not only
valued, but was intimately acquainted with, his writings.
Eusebius quotes from the work of Hegesippus a very
long account of the martyrdom of James ; [1] he refers to
Hegesippus as his authority for the statement that
Simeon was a cousin (ἀνεψιός) of Jesus, Cleophas his
father being, according to that author, the brother of
Joseph ; [2] he confirms a passage in the Epistle of Clement
by reference to Hegesippus ; [3] he quotes from Hegesippus a story regarding some members of the family of
Jesus, of the race of David, who were brought before
Domitian ; [4] he cites his narrative of the martyrdom of
Simeon, together with other matters concerning the
early Church ; [5] in another place he gives a laudatory
account of Hegesippus and his writings ; [6] shortly after
he refers to the statement of Hegesippus that he was
in Rome until the episcopate of Eleutherus,[7] and further
speaks in praise of his work, mentions his observation
on the Epistle of Clement, and quotes his remarks
about the Church in Corinth, the succession of Roman
bishops, the general state of the Church, the rise of
heresies, and other matters.[8] I mention these numerous references to Hegesippus as I have noticed them
in turning over the pages of Eusebius, but others may
very probably have escaped me. Eusebius fulfils his

[1] *H. E.* ii. 23.
[2] *Ibid.* iii. 11.
[3] *Ibid.* 16.
[4] *Ibid.* 19, 20.
[5] *Ibid.* 32.
[6] *Ibid.* iv. 8.
[7] *Ibid.* 11.
[8] *Ibid.* iv. 22.

pledge, and states what disputed works were used by Hegesippus and what he said about them, and one of these was the Gospel according to the Hebrews. He does not, however, record a single remark of any kind regarding our Gospels, and the legitimate inference, and it is the only one I care to draw, is, that Hegesippus did not say anything about them. I may simply add that, as Eusebius quotes the account of Matthew and Mark from Papias, a man of whom he expresses something like contempt, and again refers to him in confirmation of the statement of the Alexandrian Clement regarding the composition of Mark's Gospel,[1] it would be against all reason, as well as opposed to his pledge and general practice, to suppose that Eusebius would have omitted to record any information given by Hegesippus, a writer with whom he was so well acquainted, and of whom he speaks with so much respect.

I have said that Eusebius would more particularly have quoted anything with regard to the Fourth Gospel, and for those who care to go more closely into the point my reasons may be briefly given. No one can read Eusebius attentively without noting the peculiar care with which he speaks of John and his writings, and the substantially apologetic tone which he adopts in regard to them. Apart from any doubts expressed regarding the Gospel itself, the controversy as to the authenticity of the Apocalypse and second and third Epistles called by his name, with which Eusebius was so well acquainted, and the critical dilemma as to the impossibility of the same John having written both the Gospel and Apocalypse, regarding which he so fully quotes the argument of Dionysius of Alexandria,[2] evidently made him peculiarly interested in the subject, and his attention to the fourth Gospel was certainly not diminished by his recognition of the essential difference between that work and the three Synoptics. The first occasion on which he speaks of John, he records the tradition that he was banished to Patmos during the persecution under Domitian, and refers to the Apocalypse. He quotes Irenæus

---

[1] *H. E.* ii. 15.   [2] *Ibid.* vii. 25.

in support of this tradition, and the composition of the work at the close of Domitian's reign.[1] He goes on to speak of the persecution under Domitian, and quotes Hegesippus as to a command given by that Emperor to slay all the posterity of David,[2] as also Tertullian's account,[3] winding up his extracts from the historians of the time by the statement that, after Nerva succeeded Domitian, and the Senate had revoked the cruel decrees of the latter, the Apostle John returned from exile in Patmos and, according to ecclesiastical tradition, settled at Ephesus.[4] He states that John, the beloved disciple, apostle and evangelist, governed the Churches of Asia after the death of Domitian and his return from Patmos, and that he was still living when Trajan succeeded Nerva, and for the truth of this he quotes passages from Irenæus and Clement of Alexandria.[5] He then gives an account of the writings of John, and whilst asserting that the Gospel must be universally acknowledged as genuine, he says that it is rightly put last in order amongst the four, of the composition of which he gives an elaborate description. It is not necessary to quote his account of the fourth Gospel and of the occasion of its composition, which he states to have been John's receiving the other three Gospels, and, whilst admitting their truth, perceiving that they did not contain a narrative of the earlier history of Christ. For this reason, being entreated to do so, he wrote an account of the doings of Jesus before the Baptist was cast into prison. After some very extraordinary reasoning, Eusebius says that no one who carefully considers the points he mentions can think that the Gospels are at variance with each other, and he conjectures that John probably omitted the genealogies because Matthew and Luke had given them.[6] Without further anticipating what I have to say when speaking of Papias, it is clear, I think, that Eusebius, being aware of, and interested in, the peculiar difficulties connected with the writings attributed to John, not to put a still stronger case, and quoting traditions from later and consequently less weighty authorities, would certainly have recorded with more special readiness any information on the subject given by Hegesippus, whom he so frequently lays under contribution, had his writings contained any.

In regard to PAPIAS the case is still clearer. We find that Eusebius quotes his account of the composition of

---

[1] *H. E.* iii. 18.   [4] *Ibid.* 20.
[2] *Ibid.* 10, 20.   [5] *Ibid.* 23.
[3] *Ibid.* 20.   [6] *Ibid.* 24.

Gospels by Matthew and Mark,[1] although he had already given a closely similar narrative regarding Mark from Clement of Alexandria, and appealed to Papias in confirmation of it. Is it either possible or permissible to suppose that, had Papias known anything of the other two Gospels, he would not have enquired about them from the Presbyters and recorded their information ? And is it either possible or permissible to suppose that if Papias had recorded any similar information regarding the composition of the third and fourth Gospels, Eusebius would have omitted to quote it ? Certainly not ; and Dr. Lightfoot's article proves it. Eusebius had not only pledged himself to give such information, and does so in every case which we can test, but he fulfils it by actually quoting what Papias had to say about the Gospels. Even if he had been careless, his very reference to the first two Gospels must have reminded him of the claims of the rest. There are, however, special reasons which render it still more certain that had Papias had anything to tell about the Fourth Gospel,—and if there was a Fourth Gospel in his knowledge he must have had something to tell about it,—Eusebius would have recorded it. The first quotation which he makes from Papias is the passage in which the Bishop of Hierapolis states the interest with which he had enquired about the words of the Presbyters, " what John or Matthew or what any other of the disciples of the Lord said, and what Aristion and the Presbyter John, disciples of the Lord, say." [2] Eusebius observes, and particularly points out, that the name of John is twice mentioned in the passage, the former, mentioned

---

[1] I am much obliged to Dr. Lightfoot for calling my attention to the accidental insertion of the words " and the Apocalypse " (*S. R.* i. p. 483). This was a mere slip of the pen, of which no use is made, and the error is effectually corrected by my own distinct statements.

[2] *H. E.* iii. 39.

with Peter, James, and Matthew, and other Apostles, evidently being, he thinks, the Evangelist, and the latter being clearly distinguished by the designation of Presbyter. Eusebius states that this proves the truth of the assertion that there were two men of the name of John in Asia, and that two tombs were still shown at Ephesus bearing the name of John. Eusebius then proceeds to argue that probably the second of the two Johns, if not the first, was the man who saw the Revelation. What an occasion for quoting any information bearing at all on the subject from Papias, who had questioned those who had been acquainted with both! His attention is so pointedly turned to John at the very moment when he makes his quotations regarding Matthew and Mark, that I am fully warranted, both by the conclusions of Dr. Lightfoot and the peculiar circumstances of the case, in affirming that the silence of Eusebius proves that Papias said nothing about either the third or fourth Gospels.

I need not go on to discuss Dionysius of Corinth, for the same reasoning equally applies to his case. I have, therefore, only a few more words to say on the subject of Eusebius. Not content with what he intended to be destructive criticism, Dr. Lightfoot valiantly proceeds to the constructive and, " as a sober deduction from facts," makes the following statement, which he prints in italics: " *The silence of Eusebius respecting early witnesses to the Fourth Gospel is an evidence in its favour.*" [1] Now, interpreted even by the rules laid down by Dr. Lightfoot himself, what does this silence really mean? It means, not that the early writers about whom he is supposed to be silent are witnesses about anything connected with the Fourth

---

[1] *Contemporary Review*, January 1875, p. 183 [*ibid.* p. 51].

Gospel, but simply that if Eusebius noticed and did not record the mere use of that Gospel by anyone, he thereby indicates that he himself, in the fourth century, classed it amongst the undisputed books, the mere use of which he does not undertake to mention. The value of his opinion at so late a date is very small.

Professor Lightfoot next makes a vehement attack upon me in connection with " THE IGNATIAN EPISTLES," [1] which is equally abortive and limited to details. I do not intend to complain of the spirit in which the article is written, nor of its unfairness. On the whole I think that readers may safely be left to judge of the tone in which a controversy is carried on. Unfortunately, however, the perpetual accusation of misstatement brought against me in this article, and based upon minute criticism into which few care to follow, is apt to leave the impression that it is well-founded, for there is the very natural feeling in most right minds that no one would recklessly scatter such insinuations. It is this which alone makes such an attack dangerous. Now in a work like this, dealing with so many details, it must be obvious that it is not possible altogether to escape errors. A critic or opponent is of course entitled to point these out, although, if he be high-minded or even alive to his own interests, I scarcely think that he will do so in a spirit of unfair detraction. But in doing this a writer is bound to be accurate, for if he be liberal of such accusations and it can be shown that his charges are unfounded, they recoil with double force upon himself. I propose, therefore, as it is impossible for me to reply to all such attacks, to follow Professor Lightfoot and Dr. Westcott with some minuteness in their discussion

---

[1] *Contemporary Review*, February 1875, p. 337 ff. [*ibid.* p. 50 ff.]

of my treatment of the Ignatian Epistles, and once for all to show the grave misstatements to which they commit themselves.

Dr. Lightfoot does not ignore the character of the discussion upon which he enters, but it will be seen that his appreciation of its difficulty by no means inspires him with charitable emotions. He says: " The Ignatian question is the most perplexing which confronts the student of earlier Christian history. The literature is voluminous; the considerations involved are very wide, very varied, and very intricate. A writer, therefore, may well be pardoned if he betrays a want of familiarity with this subject. But in this case the reader naturally expects that the opinions at which he has arrived will be stated with some diffidence."[1] My critic objects that I express my opinions with decision. I shall here-after justify this decision, but I would here point out that the very reasons which render it difficult for Dr. Lightfoot to form a final and decisive judgment on the question make it easy for me. It requires but little logical perception to recognize that Epistles, the authen-ticity of which it is so difficult to establish, cannot have much influence as testimony for the Gospels. The statement just quoted, however, is made the base of the attack, and war is declared in the following terms :—

" The reader is naturally led to think that a writer would not use such very decided language unless he had obtained a thorough mastery of his subject; and when he finds the notes thronged with references to the most recondite sources of information, he at once credits the author with an 'exhaustive' knowledge of the literature bearing upon it. It becomes important therefore to enquire whether the writer shows that accurate acquaintance with the subject, which

---

[1] *Contemporary Review*, February 1875, p. 339 [*ibid.* p. 62].

justifies us in attaching weight to his dicta as distinguished from his arguments." [1]

This sentence shows the scope of the discussion. My dicta, however, play a very subordinate part throughout, and even if no weight be attached to them —and I have never desired that any should be—my argument would not be in the least degree affected.

The first point attacked, like most of those subsequently assailed, is one of mere critical history. I wrote: "The strongest internal, as well as other evidence, into which space forbids our going in detail, has led (1) the majority of critics to recognize the Syriac version as the most genuine form of the letters of Ignatius extant, and (2) this is admitted by most of those who nevertheless deny the authenticity of any of the epistles." [2]

Upon this Dr. Lightfoot remarks :—

"No statement could be more erroneous as a summary of the results of the Ignatian controversy since the publication of the Syriac epistles than this." [1]

It will be admitted that this is pretty "decided language" for one who is preaching "diffidence." When we come to details, however, Dr. Lightfoot admits: "Those who maintain the genuineness of the Ignatian Epistles in one or other of the two forms, may be said to be almost evenly divided on this question of priority." He seems to consider that he sufficiently shows this when he mentions five or six critics on either side; but even on this modified interpretation of my statement its correctness may be literally maintained. To the five names quoted as recognising the priority of the Syriac Epistles may be added those of Milman, Böhringer, de

---

[1] *Contemporary Review*, February 1875, p. 340 [*ibid.* p. 63].
[2] *S. R.* i. p. 263 f. I have introduced numbers for facility of reference.

Pressensé, and Dr. Tregelles, which immediately occur
to me. But I must ask upon what ground he limits my
remark to those who absolutely admit the genuineness?
I certainly do not so limit it, but affirm that a majority
prefer the three Curetonian Epistles, and that this
majority is made up partly of those who, denying the
authenticity of any of the letters, still consider the
Syriac the purest and least adulterated form of the
Epistles. This will be evident to anyone who reads
the context. With regard to the latter (2) part of the
sentence, I will at once say that "most" is a slip of
the pen for "many," which I correct in this edition.[1]
Many of those who deny or do not admit the authenticity prefer the Curetonian version. The Tübingen
school are not unanimous on the point, and there are
critics who do not belong to it. Bleek, for instance,
who does not commit himself to belief, considers the
priority of the Curetonian "im höchsten Grade wahr-
scheinlich." Volkmar, Lipsius, and Rumpf prefer them.
Dr. Lightfoot says :—

"The case of Lipsius is especially instructive, as illustrating this
point. Having at one time maintained the priority and genuineness of the Curetonian letters, he has lately, if I rightly understand
him, retracted his former opinion on both questions alike."[2]

Dr. Lightfoot, however, has not rightly understood him.
Lipsius has only withdrawn his opinion that the Syriac
letters are authentic, but whilst now asserting that in
all their forms the Ignatian Epistles are spurious, he still
maintains the priority of the Curetonian version. He
first announced this change of view emphatically in
1873, when he added : " An dem relativ grössern Alter
der syrischen Textgestalt gegenüber der kürzeren grie-

---

[1] Dr. Lightfoot says in this volume : "The reading 'most' is explained
in the preface to that edition as a misprint" (p. 63, n. 2). Not so at all. " A
slip of the pen " is a very different thing.
[2] *Contemporary Review*, February 1875, p. 341 [*ibid.* p. 64].

chischen halte ich übrigens nach wie vor fest." [1] In the very paper to which Dr. Lightfoot refers, Lipsius also again says quite distinctly : "Ich bin noch jetzt überzeugt, dass der Syrer in zahlreichen Fällen den relativ ursprünglichsten Text bewahrt hat (vgl. meine Nachweise in 'Niedner's Zeitschr.' S. 15ff)." [2] With regard to the whole of this (2) point, it must be remembered that the only matter in question is simply a shade of opinion amongst critics who deny the authenticity of the Ignatian Epistles in all forms.

Dr. Lightfoot, however, goes on " to throw some light on this point" by analysing my "general statement of the course of opinion on this subject given in an earlier passage." [3] The "light" which he throws seems to pass through so peculiar a medium, that I should be much rather tempted to call it darkness. I beg the reader to favour me with his attention to this matter, for here commences a serious attack upon the accuracy of my notes and statements, which is singularly full of error and misrepresentation. The general statement referred to and quoted is as follows :—

" These three Syriac epistles have been subjected to the severest scrutiny, and many of the ablest critics have pronounced them to be the only authentic Epistles of Ignatius, whilst others, who do not admit that even these are genuine letters emanating from Ignatius, still prefer them to the version of seven Greek epistles, and consider them the most ancient form of the letters which we possess.([1]) As early as the sixteenth century, however, the strongest doubts were expressed regarding the authenticity of any of the epistles ascribed to Ignatius. The Magdeburg Centuriators first attacked them, and Calvin declared (p. 260) them to be spurious,[1] an opinion

---

[1] *Ueber d. Urspr. u.s.w. des Christennamens,* p. 7, Anm. 1.
[2] *Zeitschr. wiss. Theol.* 1874, p. 211, Anm. 1. I should have added that the priority which Lipsius still maintains is that of the text, as Dr. Lightfoot points out in his *Apostolic Fathers* (part ii. vol. i. 1885, p. 273, n. 1), and not of absolute origin ; but this appears clearly enough in the quotations I have made.
[3] *Contemporary Review,* February 1875, p. 841 [*ibid.* p. 05].

fully shared by Chemnitz, Dallæus, and others ; and similar doubts, more or less definite, were expressed throughout the seventeenth century,([2]) and onward to comparatively recent times,([3]) although the means of forming a judgment were not then so complete as now. That the epistles were interpolated there was no doubt. Fuller examination and more comprehensive knowledge of the subject have confirmed earlier doubts, and a large mass of critics recognise that the authenticity of none of these epistles can be established, and that they can only be considered later and spurious compositions.([4]) " [1]

In the first note ([1]) on p. 259 I referred to Bunsen, Bleek, Böhringer, Cureton, Ewald, Lipsius, Milman, Ritschl, and Weiss, and Dr. Lightfoot proceeds to analyse my statements as follows : and I at once put his explanation and my text in parallel columns, italicising parts of both to call more immediate attention to the point :—

THE TRUTH.	DR. LIGHTFOOT'S STATEMENT.
Many of the ablest critics have pronounced them to be the only authentic Epistles of Ignatius, whilst others who do not admit that even these are genuine letters emanating from Ignatius, *still prefer them* to the version of seven Greek Epistles, *and consider them the most ancient form of the letters* which we possess. [1]	" These references, it will be observed, are given to illustrate *more immediately*, though perhaps not solely, the statement that writers ' *who do not admit that even these* (the Curetonian Epistles) *are genuine letters emanating from Ignatius, still prefer them* to the version of seven Greek Epistles, and consider them the most ancient form of the letters which we possess.' " [2]

It must be evident to anyone who reads the context [3] that in this sentence I am stating opinions expressed in favour of the Curetonian Epistles, and that the note, which is naturally put at the end of that sentence, must be intended to represent this favourable opinion, whether of those who absolutely maintain the authenticity or

[1] *S. R.* i. p. 259 f.
[2] *Contemporary Review*, February 1875, p. 342 [*ibid.* p. 65 f.]
[3] *S. R.* i. p. 259.

merely the relative priority. Dr. Lightfoot quietly suppresses, in his comments, the main statement of the text which the note illustrates, and then " throws light " upon the point by the following remarks :—

THE TRUTH.	DR. LIGHTFOOT'S STATEMENT.
Cureton, Bunsen, Böhringer, Ewald, Milman, Ritschl, and *Weiss* maintain both the priority and genuineness of the Syriac Epistles. *Bleek* will not commit himself to a distinct recognition of the letters in any form. Of the Vossian Epistles, he says : " Aber auch die Echtheit dieser Recension ist keineswegs sicher." He considers the priority of the Curetonian " in the highest degree probable." *Lipsius* rejects all the Epistles, as I have already said, but maintains the priority of the Syriac.	" The reader, therefore, will hardly be prepared to hear that not one of these nine writers condemns the Ignatian letters as spurious. Bleek alone leaves the matter in some uncertainty while inclining to Bunsen's view ; the other eight distinctly maintain the genuineness of the Curetonian letters." [1]

Dr. Lightfoot's statement, therefore, is a total misrepresentation of the facts, and of that mischievous kind which does most subtle injury. Not one reader in twenty would take the trouble to investigate, but would receive from such positive assertions an impression that my note was totally wrong, when in fact it is literally correct.

Continuing his analysis, Dr. Lightfoot fights almost every inch of the ground in the very same style. He cannot contradict my statement that so early as the sixteenth century the strongest doubts were expressed

---

[1] *Contemporary Review*, February 1875, p. 342. In a note Dr. Lightfoot states that my references to Lipsius are to his earlier works, where he still maintains the priority and genuineness of the Curetonian Epistles. Certainly they are so ; but in the right place, two pages further on, I refer to the writings in which he rejects the authenticity, whilst still maintaining his previous view of the priority of these letters [*ibid.* p. 66].

regarding the authenticity of any of the Epistles ascribed
to Ignatius, and that the Magdeburg Centuriators attacked
them, and Calvin declared them to be spurious,[1] but
Dr. Lightfoot says : " The criticisms of Calvin more
especially refer to those passages which were found in
the Long Recension alone." [2]   Of course only the Long
Recension was at that time known.   Rivet replies to
Campianus that Calvin's objections were not against
Ignatius but the Jesuits who had corrupted him.[3]   This
is the usual retort theological, but as I have quoted the
words of Calvin the reader may judge for himself.   Dr.
Lightfoot then says :—

"The clause which follows contains a direct misstatement.
Chemnitz did not fully share the opinion that they were spurious ;
on the contrary, he quotes them several times as authoritative ; but
he says that they 'seem to have been altered in many places to
strengthen the position of the Papal power, &c.' " [4]

Pearson's statement here quoted must be received with
reserve, for Chemnitz rather speaks sarcastically of those
who quote these Epistles as evidence.   In treating them
as ancient documents or speaking of parts of them with
respect, Chemnitz does nothing more than the Magdeburg Centuriators, but this is a very different thing from
directly ascribing them to Ignatius himself.   The Epistles
in the " Long Recension " were before Chemnitz both in
the Latin and Greek forms.   He says of them: " . . . . et
multas habent non contemnendas sententias, præsertim
sicut Græce leguntur.   Admixta vero sunt et alia non
pauca, quæ profecto non referunt gravitatem Apostoli-
cam.   Adulteratas enim jam esse illas epistolas, vel inde

[1] Calvin's expressions are : "Nihil næniis illis, quæ sub Ignatii nomine
editæ sunt, putidius.   Quo minus tolerabilis est eorum impudentia, qui
talibus larvis ad fallendum se instruunt" (*Inst. Chr. Rel.* i. 13, § 39).
[2] *Contemporary Review*, February 1875, p. 342.
[3] *Op. Theolog.* 1052, ii. p. 1085.
[4] *Contemporary Review*, February 1875, p. 342 [*ibid.* p. 60].   Dr. Lightfoot refers to Pearson's *Vindiciæ Iynat.* p. 28 (ed. Churton).

colligitur." He then shows that quotations in ancient writers purporting to be taken from the Epistles of Ignatius are not found in these extant Epistles at all, and says : " De Epistolis igitur illis Ignatii, quæ nunc ejus titulo feruntur, merito dubitamus : transformatæ enim videntur in multis locis, ad stabiliendum statum regni Pontificii." [1] Even when he speaks in favour of them he "damns them with faint praise." The whole of the discussion turns upon the word " fully," and is an instance of the minute criticism of my critic, who evidently is not directly acquainted with Chemnitz. A shade more or less of doubt or certainty in conveying the impression received from the words of a writer is scarcely worth much indignation.

Dr. Lightfoot makes a very detailed attack upon my next two notes, and here again I must closely follow him. My note ([2]) p. 260 reads as follows :—

" [2] By Bochartus, Aubertin, Blondel, Basnage, Casaubon, Cocus, Humfrey, Rivetus, Salmasius, Socinus (Faustus), Parker, Petau, &c. &c. ; cf. Jacobson, 'Patr. Apost.' i. p. xxv ; Cureton, 'Vindiciæ Ignatianæ,' 1846, appendix."

Upon this Dr. Lightfoot makes the following preliminary remarks :—

"But the most important point of all is the purpose for which they are quoted. 'Similar doubts' could only, I think, be interpreted from the context as doubts 'regarding the authenticity of any of the Epistles ascribed to Ignatius.'" [2]

As Dr. Lightfoot, in the first sentence just quoted, recognises what is " the most important point of all," it is a pity that, throughout the whole of the subsequent analysis of the references in question, he persistently ignores my very careful definition of " the purpose for

[1] *Exam. Concilii Tridentini*, 1614, i. p. 85 (misprinted 89).
[2] *Contemporary Review*, February 1875, p. 343 [*ibid.* p. 67].

which they are quoted." It is difficult, without entering into minute classifications, accurately to represent in a few words the opinions of a great number of writers, and briefly convey a fair idea of the course of critical judgment. Desirous, therefore, of embracing a large class—for both this note and the next, with mere difference of epoch, illustrate the same statement in the text—and not to overstate the case on my own side, I used what seemed to me a very moderate phrase, decreasing the force of the opinion of those who positively rejected the Epistles, and not unfairly representing the hesitation of those who did not fully accept them. I said, then, in guarded terms—and I italicise the part which Dr. Lightfoot chooses to suppress—that "similar *doubts, more or less definite*," were expressed by the writers referred to.

Dr. Lightfoot admits that Bochart directly condemns one Epistle, and would probably have condemned the rest also ; that Aubertin, Blondel, Basnage, R. Parker, and Saumaise actually rejected all ; and that Cook pronounces them " either supposititious or shamefully corrupted." So far, therefore, there can be no dispute. I will now take the rest in succession. Dr. Lightfoot says that Humfrey " considers that they have been interpolated and mutilated, but he believes them genuine in the main." Dr. Lightfoot has so completely warped the statement in the text, that he seems to demand nothing short of a total condemnation of the Epistles in the note, but had I intended to say that Humfrey and all of these writers definitely rejected the whole of the Epistles I should not have limited myself to merely saying that they expressed " *doubts* more or less definite," which Humfrey does. Dr. Lightfoot says that Socinus " denounces corruptions and anachronisms, but so far as I can see does not question a nucleus of genuine matter."

His very denunciations, however, are certainly the expression of " doubts, more or less definite." " Casaubon, so far from rejecting them altogether," Dr. Lightfoot says, " promises to defend the antiquity of some of the Epistles with new arguments." But I have never affirmed that he " rejected them altogether." Casaubon died before he fulfilled the promise referred to, so that we cannot determine what arguments he might have used. I must point out, however, that the antiquity does not necessarily involve the authenticity of a document. With regard to Rivet the case is different. I had overlooked the fact that in a subsequent edition of the work referred to, after receiving Archbishop Usher's edition of the Short Recension, he had given his adhesion to " that form of the Epistles." [1] This fact is also mentioned by Pearson, and I ought to have observed it.[2] Petau, the last of the writers referred to, says : " Equidem haud abnuerim epistolas illius varie interpolatas et quibusdam additis mutatas, ac depravatas fuisse : tum aliquas esse supposititias : verum nullas omnino ab Ignatio Epistolas esse scriptas, id vero nimium temere affirmari sentio." · He then goes on to mention the recent publication of the Vossian Epistles and the version of Usher, and the learned Jesuit Father has no more decided opinion to express than : " ut hæc prudens, ac justa suspicio sit, illas esse genuinas Ignatii epistolas, quas antiquorum consensus illustribus testimoniis commendatas ac approbatas reliquit." [3]

The next note (³), p. 260, was only separated from the preceding for convenience of reference, and Dr. Lightfoot quotes and comments upon it as follows :—

" The next note (³), p. 260, is as follows :—

---

[1] *Critici Sacri*, lib. ii. cap. 1 ; *Op. Theolog.* 1652, ii. p. 1086.
[2] *Vind. Ignat.* 1672, p. 14 f. ; Jacobson, *Patr. Apost.* i. p. xxxviii.
[3] *Op. de Theolog. Dogmat., De Eccles. Hierarch.* v. 8 § 1, edit. Venetiis, 1757, vol. vii.

" ' [Wotton, *Præf. Clem. R. Epp.* 1718] ; J. Owen, *Enquiry into Original Nature, &c., Evang. Church, Works,* ed. Russel, 1826, vol. xx. p. 147 ; Oudin, *Comm. de Script. Eccles.* &c. 1722, p. 88 ; Lampe, *Comm. analyt. ex Evang. Joan.* 1724, i. p. 184 ; Lardner, *Credibility,* &c., *Works,* ii. p. 68 f. ; Beausobre, *Hist. Crit. de Manichée,* &c. 1734, i. p. 378, note 3 ; Ernesti, *N. Theol. Biblioth.* 1761, ii. p. 489 ; [Mosheim, *De Rebus Christ.* p. 159 f.] ; Weismann, *Introd. in Memorab. Eccles.* 1745, i. p. 137 ; Heumann, *Conspect. Reipub. Lit.* 1763, p. 492 ; Schrœckh, *Chr. Kirchengesch.* 1775, ii. p. 341 ; Griesbach, *Opuscula Academ.* 1824, i. p. 26 ; Rosenmüller, *Hist. Interpr. Libr. Sacr. in Eccles.* 1795, i. p. 116 ; Semler, *Paraphr. in Epist II. Petri.* 1784, *Præf.* ; Kestner, *Comm. de Eusebii H. E. condit.* 1816, p. 63 ; Henke, *Allg. Gesch. chr. Kirche,* 1818, i. p. 96 ; Neander, *K. G.* 1843, ii. p. 1140 [cf. i. p. 327, Anm. 1] ; Baumgarten-Crusius, *Lehrb. chr. Dogmengesch.* 1832, p. 83 ; cf. *Comp. chr. Dogmengesch.* 1840, p. 79 ; [Niedner, *Gesch. chr. K.* p. 196 ; Thiersch, *Die K. im ap. Zeit.* p. 322 ; Hagenbach, *K. G.* i. p. 115 f.] ; cf. Cureton, *Vind. Ign. Append.* ; Ziegler, *Versuch eine prag. Gesch. d. kirchl. Verfassungsformen, u.s.w.* 1798, p. 16 ; J. E. C. Schmidt, *Versuch üb. d. gedopp. Recens. d. Br. S. Ignat.,* in Henke's *Mag. f. Rel. Phil.* u.s.w. [1795 ; cf. *Biblioth. f. Krit.* u.s.w., *N. T.* i. p 463 ff. *Urspr. kath. Kirche,* II. i. p. 1 f.] ; *Handbuch Chr. K. G.* i. p. 200.'

" The brackets are not the author's, but my own.

" This is doubtless one of those exhibitions of learning which have made such a deep impression on the reviewers. Certainly, as it stands, this note suggests a thorough acquaintance with all the by-paths of the Ignatian literature, and seems to represent the gleanings of many years' reading. It is important to observe, however, that every one of these references, except those which I have included in brackets, is given in the appendix to Cureton's 'Vindiciæ Ignatianæ,' where the passages are quoted in full. Thus two-thirds of this elaborate note might have been compiled in ten minutes. Our author has here and there transposed the order of the quotations, and confused it by so doing, for it is chronological in Cureton. But what purpose was served by thus importing into his notes a mass of borrowed and unsorted references ? And, if he thought fit to do so, why was the key-reference to Cureton buried among the rest, so that it stands in immediate connection with some additional references on which it has no bearing ? " [1]

---

[1] *Contemporary Review,* February 1875, p. 343 f. [*ibid.* p. 67 f.]

I do not see any special virtue in the amount of time which might suffice, under some circumstances, to compile a note, although it is here advanced as an important point to observe, but I call attention to the unfair spirit in which Dr. Lightfoot's criticisms are made. I ask every just-minded reader to consider what right any critic has to insinuate, if not directly to say, that, because some of the references in a note are also given by Cureton, I simply took them from him, and thus " imported into my notes a mass of borrowed and unsorted references," and further to insinuate that I " here and there transposed the order" apparently to conceal the source ? This is a kind of criticism which I very gladly relinquish entirely to my high-minded and reverend opponent. Now, as full quotations are given in Cureton's appendix, I should have been perfectly entitled to take references from it, had I pleased, and for the convenience of many readers I distinctly indicate Cureton's work, in the note, as a source to be compared. The fact is, however, that I did not take the references from Cureton, but in every case derived them from the works themselves, and if the note " seems to represent the gleanings of many years' reading," it certainly does not misrepresent the fact, for I took the trouble to make myself acquainted with the " by-paths of Ignatian literature." Now in analysing the references in this note it must be borne in mind that they illustrate the statement that " *doubts, more or less definite*," continued to be expressed regarding the Ignatian Epistles. I am much obliged to Dr. Lightfoot for drawing my attention to Wotton. His name is the first in the note, and it unfortunately was the last in a list on another point in my note-book, immediately preceding this one, and was by mistake included in it. I also frankly give up Weismann, whose doubts I find I had exaggerated, and proceed to examine Dr. Lightfoot's further statements. He says that Thiersch uses the Curetonian as genuine, and that his only doubt is whether he ought not to accept the Vossian. Thiersch, however, admits that he cannot quote either the seven or the three Epistles as genuine. He says distinctly : " These three Syriac Epistles lie under the suspicion that they are not an older text, but merely an epitome of the seven, for the other notes found in the same MS. seem to be excerpts. But on the other hand, the doubts regarding the genuineness of the seven Epistles, in the form in which they are known since Usher's time, are not yet entirely removed. For no MS. has yet been found which contains *only* the seven Epistles attested by Eusebius, a MS. such as lay before Eusebius." [1] Thiersch, therefore, does express " doubts, more or less definite." Dr. Lightfoot then continues : " Of the rest a considerable number, as, for instance, Lardner, Beausobre, Schrœckh, Griesbach, Kestner, Neander, and Baumgarten-Crusius, *with different degrees of certainty or uncertainty*, pronounce themselves in favour of a genuine nucleus." [2] The words which I have italicised are a mere paraphrase of my words descriptive of the doubts entertained. I must point out that a leaning towards belief in a genuine " nucleus " on the part of some of these writers, by no means excludes the expression of " *doubts, more or less definite*," which is all I quote them for. I will take each name in order.

Lardner says : " But whether the smaller (Vossian Epistles) themselves are the genuine writings of Ignatius, bishop of Antioch, is a question that has been much disputed, and has employed the pens of the

---

[1] *Die Kirche im ap. Zeit.* p. 322.
[2] *Contemporary Review*, February 1875, p. 344 f. [*ibid.* p. 63.]

ablest critics. And whatever positiveness some
may have shown on either side, I must own I have
found it a very difficult question." The opinion
which he expresses finally is merely: "it appears
to me *probable*, that they are *for the main part*
the genuine epistles of Ignatius."

Beausobre says: "Je ne veux, ni défendre, ni combattre
l'authenticité des *Lettres de St. Ignace*. Si elles
ne sont pas véritables, elles ne laissent pas d'être
fort anciennes; et l'opinion, qui me paroit la plus
raisonnable, est que les plus pures ont été inter-
polées."

Schrœckh says that along with the favourable considerations for the shorter (Vossian) Epistles "many
doubts arise which make them suspicious." He
proceeds to point out many grave difficulties, and
anachronisms which cast doubt both on individual
epistles and upon the whole, and he remarks that
a very common way of evading these and other
difficulties is to affirm that all the passages which
cannot be reconciled with the mode of thought of
Ignatius are interpolations of a later time. He
concludes with the pertinent observation: "However probable this is, it nevertheless remains as
difficult to prove which are the interpolated passages." In fact it would be difficult to point out
any writer who more thoroughly doubts, without
definitely rejecting, all the Epistles.

Griesbach and *Kestner* both express "doubts more or
less definite," but to make sufficient extracts to
illustrate this would occupy too much space.

Neander.—Dr. Lightfoot has been misled by the short
extract from the English translation of the first
edition of Neander's History given by Cureton in
his Appendix, has not attended to the brief German

quotation from the second edition, and has not examined the original at all, or he would have seen that, so far from pronouncing "in favour of a genuine nucleus," Neander might well have been classed by me amongst those who distinctly reject the Ignatian Epistles, instead of being moderately quoted amongst those who merely express doubt. Neander says : "As the account of the martyrdom of Ignatius is very suspicious, so also the Epistles which suppose the correctness of this suspicious legend do not bear throughout the impress of a distinct individuality, and of a man of that time who is addressing his last words to the communities. A hierarchical purpose is not to be mistaken." In an earlier part of the work he still more emphatically says that, " in the so-called Ignatian Epistles," he recognises a decided " design " (*Absichtlichkeit*), and then he continues : " As the tradition regarding the journey of Ignatius to Rome, there to be cast to the wild beasts, seems to me for the above-mentioned reasons very suspicious, his Epistles, which presuppose the truth of this tradition, can no longer inspire me with faith in their authenticity." [1] He goes on to state additional grounds for disbelief.

Baumgarten-Crusius stated in one place, in regard to the seven Epistles, that it is no longer possible to ascertain how much of the extant may have formed part of the original Epistles, and in a note he excepts only the passages quoted by the Fathers. He seems to agree with Semler and others that the two Recensions are probably the result of manipulations of the original, the shorter form being more in ecclesiastical, the longer in dogmatic, interest.

[1] *K. G.* 1842, i. p. 327, Anm. 1.

Some years later he remarked that enquiries into the Epistles, although not yet concluded, had rather tended towards the earlier view that the Shorter Recension was more original than the Long, but that even the shorter may have suffered, if not from manipulations (*Ueberarbeitungen*), from interpolations. This very cautious statement, it will be observed, is wholly relative, and does not in the least modify the previous conclusion that the original material of the letters cannot be ascertained.

Dr. Lightfoot's objections regarding these seven writers are thoroughly unfounded, and in most cases glaringly erroneous.

He proceeds to the next " note (^{4}) " with the same unhesitating vigour, and characterises it as "equally unfortunate." Wherever it has been possible, Dr. Lightfoot has succeeded in misrepresenting the "purpose" of my notes, although he has recognised how important it is to ascertain this correctly, and in this instance he has done so again. I will put my text and his explanation, upon the basis of which he analyses the note, in juxtaposition, italicising part of my own statement which he altogether disregards :—

	DR. LIGHTFOOT.
"Further examination and more comprehensive knowledge of the subject have confirmed earlier doubts, and a large mass of critics recognise *that the authenticity of none* of these Epistles *can be established*, and that they can only be considered later and spurious compositions."	"References to twenty authorities are then given, as belonging to the 'large mass of critics' who recognise that the Ignatian Epistles 'can only be considered later and spurious compositions.' " [1]

---

[1] *Contemporary Review*, February 1875, p. 345 [*ibid.* p. 69].

There are here, in order to embrace a number of references, two approximate states of opinion represented: the first, which leaves the Epistles in permanent doubt, as sufficient evidence is not forthcoming to establish their authenticity; and the second, which positively pronounces them to be spurious. Out of the twenty authorities referred to, Dr. Lightfoot objects to six as contradictory or not confirming what he states to be the purpose of the note. He seems to consider that a reservation for the possibility of a genuine substratum which cannot be defined invalidates my reference. I maintain, however, that it does not. It is quite possible to consider that the authenticity of the extant letters cannot be established without denying that there may have been some original nucleus upon which these actual documents may have been based. I will analyse the six references.

Bleek.—Dr. Lightfoot says: "Of these Bleek (already cited in a previous note) expresses no definite opinion."

Dr. Lightfoot omits to mention that I do not refer to Bleek directly, but by "Cf." merely request consideration of his opinions. I have already partly stated Bleek's view. After pointing out some difficulties, he says generally: "It comes to this, that the origin of the Ignatian Epistles themselves is still very doubtful." He refuses to make use of a passage because it is only found in the Long Recension, and another which occurs in the Shorter Recension he does not consider evidence, because, first, he says, "The authenticity of this Recension also is by no means certain," and, next, the Cureton Epistles discredit the others. "Whether this Recension (the Curetonian) is more original than the shorter Greek is certainly not altogether certain, but . . . . in the highest degree probable." In another place he refuses to make use of reminiscences in the "Ignatian Epistles," "because it is still very doubtful how the case stands as regards the authenticity and integrity of these Ignatian Epistles themselves, in the different Recensions in which we possess them." [1]   In fact he did not consider that their authenticity could be established. I do not, however, include him here at all.

Gfrörer.—Dr. Lightfoot, again, omits to state that I do not cite this writer like the others, but by a " Cf." merely suggest a reference to his remarks.

Harless, according to Dr. Lightfoot, "avows that he must ' decidedly reject with the most considerable critics of older and more recent times ' the opinion maintained by certain persons that the Epistles are ' altogether spurious,' and proceeds to treat a passage as genuine because it stands in the Vossian letters as well as in the Long Recension."

This is a mistake. Harless quotes a passage in connection with Paul's Epistle to the Ephesians with the distinct remark : " In this case the disadvantage of the uncertainty regarding the Recensions is *in part* removed through the circumstance that both Recensions have the passage." He recognises that the completeness of the proof that ecclesiastical tradition goes back beyond the time of Marcion is somewhat wanting from the uncertainty regarding the text of Ignatius. He did not, in fact, venture to consider the Ignatian Epistles evidence even for the first half of the second century.

Schliemann, Dr. Lightfoot states, " says that ' the external testimonies oblige him to recognise a genuine

[1] *Einl. N. T.* pp. 144 f., 233.

substratum,' though he is not satisfied with either existing recension."

Now what Schliemann says is this : "Certainly neither the Shorter and still less the Longer Recension in which we possess these Epistles can lay claim to authenticity. Only if we must, nevertheless, without doubt suppose a genuine substratum," &c. In a note he adds : "The external testimonies oblige me to recognise a genuine substratum—Polycarp already speaks of the same in Ch. xiii. of his Epistle. But that in their present form they do not proceed from Ignatius the contents sufficiently show."

Hase, according to Dr. Lightfoot, "commits himself to no opinion."

If he does not deliberately and directly do so, he indicates what that opinion is with sufficient clearness. The Long Recension, he says, bears the marks of later manipulation, and excites suspicion of an invention in favour of Episcopacy, and the shorter text is not fully attested either. The Curetonian Epistles with the shortest and least hierarchical text give the impression of an epitome. "But even if no authentic kernel lay at the basis of these Epistles, yet they would be a significant document at latest out of the middle of the second century." These last words are a clear admission of his opinion that the authenticity cannot be established.

Lechler candidly confesses that he commenced with a prejudice in favour of the authenticity of the Epistles in the Shorter Recension, but on reading them through, he says that an impression unfavourable to their authenticity was produced upon him which he had not been able to shake off. He proceeds to point out their internal improbability, and other difficulties connected with the supposed journey, which make it "still more improbable that Ignatius himself can really have written these Epistles in this situation." Lechler does not consider that the Curetonian Epistles strengthen the case; and although he admits that he cannot congratulate himself on the possession of "certainty and cheerfulness of conviction" of the inauthenticity of the Ignatian Epistles, he at least very clearly justifies the affirmation that the authenticity cannot be established.

Now what has been the result of this minute and prejudiced attack upon my notes? Out of nearly seventy critics and writers in connection with what is admitted to be one of the most intricate questions of Christian literature, it appears that—much to my regret—I have inserted one name totally by accident, overlooked that the doubts of another had been removed by the subsequent publication of the Short Recension and consequently erroneously classed him, and I withdraw a third whose doubts I consider that I have overrated. Mistakes to this extent in dealing with such a mass of references, or a difference of a shade more or less in the representation of critical opinions, not always clearly expressed, may, I hope, be excusable, and I can truly say that I am only too glad to correct such errors. On the other hand, a critic who attacks such references, in such a tone, and with such wholesale accusations of "misstatement" and "misrepresentation," was bound to be accurate, and I have shown that Dr. Lightfoot is not only inaccurate in matters of fact, but unfair in his statements of my purpose. I am happy, however, to be able to make use of his own words and say: "I may perhaps have fallen into some errors of detail, though I have endeavoured to avoid them, but the main conclusions are, I believe, irrefragable." [1]

There are further misstatements made by Dr. Lightfoot to which I must briefly refer before turning to other matters. He says, with unhesitating boldness :—

"One highly important omission is significant. There is no mention, from first to last, of the Armenian version. Now it happens that this version (so far as regards the documentary evidence) *has been felt to be the key to the position, and around it the battle has raged fiercely since its publication.* One who (like our author) maintains the priority of the Curetonian letters, was especially bound to give it some consideration, for it furnishes the most formidable argument to his opponents. This version was given to the world by Petermann in 1849, the same year in which Cureton's later work, the *Corpus Ignatianum*, appeared, and therefore was unknown to him. Its *bearing occupies a more or less prominent place in all, or nearly all, the writers who have specially discussed the Ignatian question during the last quarter of a century. This is true of Lipsius and Weiss and Hilgenfeld and Uhlhorn, whom he cites, not less than of Merx and Denzinger and Zahn, whom he neglects to cite.*" [2]

Now first as regards the facts. I do not maintain the priority of the Curetonian Epistles in this book myself; indeed I express no personal opinion whatever regarding them which is not contained in that general declaration of belief, the decision of which excites the wrath of my diffident critic, that the Epistles in no form have " any value as evidence for an earlier period than the end of the second or beginning of the third century, even if they have any value at all." I merely represent the opinion of others regarding those Epistles. Dr. Lightfoot very greatly exaggerates the importance attached to the Armenian version, and I call special attention to the passages in the above quotation which

I have taken the liberty of italicising. I venture to say emphatically that, so far from being considered the "key of the position," this version has, with some exceptions, played a most subordinate and insignificant part in the controversy, and as Dr. Lightfoot has expressly mentioned certain writers, I will state how the case stands with regard to them. Weiss, Lipsius, Uhlhorn, Merx, and Zahn certainly " more or less prominently" deal with them. Denzinger, however, only refers to Petermann's publication, which appeared while his own *brochure* was passing through the press, in a short note at the end, and in again writing on the Ignatian question, two years after,[1] he does not even allude to the Armenian version. Beyond the barest historical reference to Petermann's work, Hilgenfeld does not discuss the Armenian version at all. So much for the writers actually mentioned by Dr. Lightfoot.

As for " the writers who have specially discussed the Ignatian question during the last quarter of a century :" Cureton apparently did not think it worth while to add anything regarding the Armenian version of Petermann after its appearance ; Bunsen refutes Petermann's arguments in a few pages of his "Hippolytus;"[2] Baur, who wrote against Bunsen and the Curetonian letters, and, according to Dr. Lightfoot's representation, should have found this " the most formidable argument" against them, does not anywhere, subsequent to their publication, even allude to the Armenian Epistles ; Ewald, in a note of a couple of lines,[3] refers to Petermann's Epistles as identical with a post-Eusebian manipulated form of the Epistles which he mentions in a sentence in his text; Dressel devotes a few unfavourable

[1] *Theolog. Quartalschrift*, 1851, p. 389 ff.
[2] *Hippolytus and his Age*, 1852, i. p. 60, note, iv. p. vi ff.
[3] *Gesch. d. V. Isr.* vii. p. 391, Anm. 1.

lines to them;[1] Hefele[2] supports them at somewhat greater length; but Bleek, Volkmar, Tischendorf, Böhringer, Scholten, and others have not thought them worthy of special notice; at any rate none of these nor any other writers of any weight have, so far as I am aware, introduced them into the controversy at all.

The argument itself did not seem to me of sufficient importance to drag into a discussion already too long and complicated, and I refer the reader to Bunsen's reply to it, from which, however, I may quote the following lines :—

"But it appears to me scarcely serious to say : there are the Seven Letters in Armenian, and I maintain, they prove that Cureton's text is an incomplete extract, because, I think, I have found some Syriac idioms in the Armenian text ! Well, if that is not a joke, it simply proves, according to ordinary logic, that the Seven Letters must have once been translated into Syriac. But how can it prove that the Greek original of this supposed Syriac version is the genuine text, and not an interpolated and partially forged one ?"[3]

Dr. Lightfoot blames me for omitting to mention this argument, on the ground that " a discussion which, while assuming the priority of the Curetonian letters, ignores this version altogether, has omitted a vital problem of which it was bound to give an account." Now all this is sheer misrepresentation. I do not assume the priority of the Curetonian Epistles, and I examine all the passages contained in the seven Greek Epistles which have any bearing upon our Gospels.

Passing on to another point, I say :—

" Seven Epistles have been selected out of fifteen

---

[1] *Patr. Apost. Proleg.* 1863, p. xxx.
[2] *Patr. Apost.* ed. 4th, 1855. In a review of Denzinger's work in the *Theolog. Quartalschrift*, 1849, p. 683 ff., Hefele devotes eight lines to the Armenian version (p. 685 f.)
[3] *Hippolytus*, 1852, i. p. 60, note. Cf. iv. p. vi ff.

extant, all equally purporting to be by Ignatius, simply because only that number were mentioned by Eusebius." [1]

Another passage is also quoted by Dr. Lightfoot, which will be found a little further on, where it is taken for facility of reference. Upon this he writes as follows :—

"This attempt to confound the seven Epistles mentioned by Eusebius with the other confessedly spurious Epistles, as if they presented themselves to us with the same credentials, ignores all the important facts bearing on the question. (1) Theodoret, a century after Eusebius, betrays no knowledge of any other Epistles, and there is no distinct trace of the use of the confessedly spurious Epistles till late in the sixth century at the earliest. (2) The confessedly spurious Epistles differ widely in style from the seven Epistles, and betray the same hand which interpolated the seven Epistles. In other words, they clearly formed part of the Long Recension in the first instance. (3) They abound in anachronisms which point to an age later than Eusebius, as the date of their composition." [2]

Although I do not really say in the above that no other pleas are advanced in favour of the seven Epistles, I contend that, reduced to its simplest form, the argument for that special number rests mainly, if not altogether, upon their mention by Eusebius. The very first reason (1) advanced by Dr. Lightfoot to refute me is a practical admission of the correctness of my statement, for the eight Epistles are put out of court because even Theodoret, a century after Eusebius, does not betray any knowledge of them, but the "silence of Eusebius," the earlier witness, is infinitely more important, and it merely receives some increase of significance from the silence of Theodoret. Suppose, however, that Eusebius had referred to any of them, how changed their position would have been! The Epistles referred

[1] *S. R.* i. p. 264.
[2] *Contemporary Review*, February 1875, p. 347 [*ibid.* p. 72].

to would have attained the exceptional distinction
which his mention has conferred upon the rest. The
fact is, moreover, that, throughout the controversy, the
two divisions of Epistles are commonly designated the
" præ- " and " post-Eusebian," making him the turning-
point of the controversy. Indeed, further on, Dr. Lightfoot himself admits : " The testimony of Eusebius first
differentiates them." [1] The argument (2 and 3) that
the eight rejected Epistles betray anachronisms and interpolations, is no refutation of my statement, for the
same accusation is brought by the majority of critics
against the Vossian Epistles.

The fourth and last argument seems more directly
addressed to a second paragraph quoted by Dr. Lightfoot, to which I refer above, and which I have reserved
till now, as it requires more detailed notice. It is this :—

" It is a total mistake to suppose that the seven Epistles mentioned by Eusebius have been transmitted to us in any special way.
These Epistles are mixed up in the Medicean and corresponding
ancient Latin MSS. with the other eight Epistles, universally pronounced to be spurious, without distinction of any kind, and all
have equal honour." [2]

I will at once give Dr. Lightfoot's comment on this, in
contrast with the statement of a writer equally distinguished for learning and orthodoxy—Dr. Tregelles :—

DR. LIGHTFOOT.	DR. TREGELLES.
(4) " It is not strictly true that the seven Epistles are mixed up with the confessedly spurious Epistles. In the Greek and Latin MSS., as also in the Armenian version, the spurious Epistles come after the others ; and the circumstance, combined with the facts already mentioned, plainly shows	" It is a mistake to think of *seven* Ignatian Epistles in Greek having been *transmitted* to us, for no such seven exist, except through their having been selected by *editors* from the Medicean MS. which contains so much that is confessedly spurious ;—a fact which some who imagine a diplo-

that they were a later addition, borrowed from the Long Recension to complete the body of Ignatian letters."[1]

matic transmission of *seven* have overlooked."[2]

I will further quote the words of Cureton, for, as Dr. Lightfoot advances nothing but assertions, it is well to meet him with the testimony of others rather than the mere reiteration of my own statement. Cureton says :—

"Again, there is another circumstance which will naturally lead us to look with some suspicion upon the recension of the Epistles of St. Ignatius, as exhibited in the Medicean MS., and in the ancient Latin version corresponding with it, which is, that the Epistles presumed to be the genuine production of that holy Martyr are mixed up with others, which are almost universally allowed to be spurious. Both in the Greek and Latin MSS. all these are placed upon the same footing, and no distinction is drawn between them ; and the only ground which has hitherto been assumed for their separation has been the specification of some of them by Eusebius and his omission of any mention of the others."[3]

"The external evidence from the testimony of manuscripts in favour of the rejected Greek Epistles, with the exception of that to the Philippians, is certainly greater than that in favour of those which have been received. They are found in all the manuscripts, both Greek and Latin, in the same form ; while the others exhibit two distinct and very different recensions, if we except the Epistle to Polycarp, in which the variations are very few. Of these two recensions the shorter has been most generally received : the circumstance of its being shorter seems much to have influenced its reception ; and the text of the Medicean Codex and of the two copies of the corresponding Latin version belonging to Caius College, Cambridge,

---

[1] *Contemporary Review*, February 1875, p. 347 [*ibid.* p. 72 f.] Dr. Lightfoot makes the following important admission in a note: "The Roman Epistle indeed has been separated from its companions, and is embedded in the Martyrology which stands at the end of this collection in the Latin Version, where doubtless it stood also in the Greek, before the MS. of this latter was mutilated. Otherwise the Vossian Epistles come together, and *are followed* by the confessedly spurious Epistles in the Greek and Latin MSS. In the Armenian all the Vossian Epistles are together, and the confessedly spurious Epistles follow. See Zahn, *Ignatius von Antiochien*, p. 111."
[2] Note to Horne's *Int. to the Holy Scriptures*, 12th ed. 1869, iv. p. 332, note 1. The italics are in the original.
[3] *The Ancient Syrian Version*, &c. 1845, p. xxiv f.

and Corpus Christi College, Oxford, has been adopted. . . . In all
these there is no distinction whatever drawn between the former
and latter Epistles: all are placed upon the same basis; and there
is no ground whatever to conclude either that the arranger of the
Greek recension or the translator of the Latin version esteemed one
to be better or more genuine than another.   Nor can any prejudice
result to the Epistles to the Tarsians, to the Antiochians, and to
Hero, from the circumstance of their being placed after the others
in the collection; for they are evidently arranged in chronological
order, and rank after the rest as having been written from Philippi,
at which place Ignatius is said to have arrived after he had de-
spatched the previous Letters.   So far, therefore, as the evidence of
all the existing copies, Latin as well as Greek, of both the recensions
is to be considered, it is certainly in favour of the rejected Epistles,
rather than of those which have been retained." [1]

Proceeding from counter-statements to actual facts,
I will very briefly show the order in which these Epistles
have been found in some of the principal MSS.   One of
the earliest published was the ancient Latin version of
eleven Epistles edited by J. Faber Stapulensis in 1498,
which was at least quoted in the ninth century, and
which in the subjoined table I shall mark A,[2] and
which also exhibits the order of Cod. Vat. 859, assigned
to the eleventh century.[3]   The next (B) is a Greek MS.
edited by Valentinus Pacæus in 1557,[4] and the order at
the same time represents that of the Cod. Pal. 150.[5]
The third (C) is the ancient Latin translation, referred
to above, published by Archbishop Usher.[6]   The fourth
(D) is the celebrated Medicean MS. assigned to the
eleventh century, and published by Vossius in 1646.[7]
This also represents the order of the Cod. Casanatensis
G. V. 14.[8]   I italicise the rejected Epistles :—

[1] *Corpus Ignat.* p. 338.   [2] *Ibid.* p. ii.
[3] Dressel, *Patr. Ap.* p. lvi.   [4] Cureton, *Corp. Ign.* p. iii.
[5] Dressel, *Patr. Ap.* p. lvii f.   [6] Cureton, *Corp. Ignat.* p. vii f.
[7] *Ibid.* p. xi; Dressel, *Patr. Ap.* p. xxxi; cf. p. lxii; Jacobson, *Patr.
Ap.* i. p. lxxiii; Vossius, *Ep. gen. S. Ign. Mart.*, Amstel. 1646.
[8] Dressel, *Patr. Ap.* p. lxi.

A. FABER STAP.	B. VAL. PACÆUS.	C. USHER.	D. VOSSIUS.
1. Trallians	*Mar. Cass.*	Smyrn.	Smyrn.
2. Magn.	Trallians	Polycarp	Polycarp
3. *Tarsians*	Magnes.	Ephes.	Ephes.
4. *Philip.*	*Tarsians*	Magnes.	Magnes.
5. Philad.	*Philip.*	Philad.	Philad.
6. Smyrn.	Philad.	Trallians	Trallians
7. Polycarp	Smyrn.	*Mar. ad Ign.*	*Mar. ad Ign.*
8. *Antioch.*	Polycarp	*Ign. ad Mar.*	*Ign. ad Mar.*
9. *Hero*	*Antioch.*	*Tarsians*	*Tarsians*
10. Ephes.	*Hero*	*Antioch.*	
11. Romans	Ephes.	*Hero*	
12.	Romans	*Mart. Ign.*	
13.		Romans	

I have given the order in MSS. containing the " Long
Recension " as well as the Vossian, because, however
much some may desire to exclude them, the variety of
arrangement is notable, and presents features which
have an undeniable bearing upon this question. Taking
the Vossian MS., it is obvious that, without any distinction whatever between the genuine and the spurious,
it contains three of the false Epistles, and *does not contain the so-called genuine Epistle to the Romans at all.*
The Epistle to the Romans, in fact, is, to use Dr. Lightfoot's own expression, " embedded in the Martyrology,"
which is as spurious as any of the epistles. This circumstance alone would justify the assertion which Dr.
Lightfoot contradicts.

I must now, in order finally to dispose of this matter
of notes, turn for a short time to consider objections
raised by Dr. Westcott. Whilst I have to thank him
for greater courtesy, I regret that I must point out
serious errors into which he has fallen in his statements
regarding my references, which, as matters of fact,
admit of practical test. Before proceeding to them I

may make one or two general observations. Dr. Westcott says :—

> "I may perhaps express my surprise that a writer who is quite
> capable of thinking for himself should have considered it worth his
> while to burden his pages with lists of names and writings, arranged,
> for the most part, alphabetically, which have in very many cases no
> value whatever for a scholar, while they can only oppress the general
> reader with a vague feeling that all 'profound' critics are on one side.
> The questions to be discussed must be decided by evidence and by
> argument and not by authority.".[1]

Now the fact is that hitherto, in England, argument
and evidence have almost been ignored in connection
with the great question discussed in this work, and it
has practically been decided by the authority of the
Church, rendered doubly potent by force of habit and
transmitted reverence. The orthodox works usually
written on the subject have, to a very great extent, suppressed the objections raised by a mass of learned and
independent critics, or treated them as insignificant,
and worthy of little more than a passing word of pious
indignation. At the same time, therefore, that I endeavour, to the best of my ability, to decide these
questions by evidence and argument, in opposition to
mere ecclesiastical authority, I refer readers desirous
of further pursuing the subject to works where they
may find them discussed. I must be permitted to add,
that I do not consider I uselessly burden my pages by
references to critics who confirm the views in the text
or discuss them, for it is right that earnest thinkers
should be told the state of opinion, and recognise that
belief is not so easy and matter-of-course a thing as
they have been led to suppose, or the unanimity quite
so complete as English divines have often seemed to
represent it. Dr. Westcott, however, omits to state

---

[1] "A Few Words on 'Supernatural Religion,'" pref. to *Hist. of the
Canon*, 4th ed. 1874, p. xix.

that I as persistently refer to writers who oppose, as to those who favour, my own conclusions.

Dr. Westcott proceeds to make the accusation which I now desire to investigate. He says :—

"Writers are quoted as holding on independent grounds an opinion which is involved in their characteristic assumptions. And more than this, the references are not unfrequently actually misleading. One example will show that I do not speak too strongly."[1]

Dr. Westcott has scrutinised this work with great minuteness, and, as I shall presently explain, he has selected his example with evident care. The idea of illustrating the vast mass of references in these volumes by a single instance is somewhat startling, but to insinuate that a supposed contradiction pointed out in one note runs through the whole work, as he does, if I rightly understand his subsequent expressions, is scarcely worthy of Dr. Westcott, although I am sure he does not mean to be unfair. The example selected is as follows :—

" ' It has been demonstrated that Ignatius was not sent to Rome at all, but suffered martyrdom in Antioch itself on the 20th December, A.D. 115,[3] when he was condemned to be cast to wild beasts in the amphitheatre, in consequence of the fanatical excitement produced by the earthquake which took place on the 13th of that month.[4]'[2]

" ' The references in support of these statements are the following :—

" ' [3] Baur, *Urspr. d. Episc., Tüb. Zeitschr. f. Theol.* 1838, H. 3, p. 155, Anm. ; Bretschneider, *Probabilia,* &c. p. 185 ; Bleek, *Einl. N. T.* p. 144 ; Guericke, *Handbuch, K. G.* i. p. 148; Hagenbach, *K. G.* i. p. 113 f. ; Davidson, *Introd. N. T.* i. p. 19 ; Mayerhoff, *Einl. petr. Schr.* p. 79 ; Scholten, *Die ält. Zeugnisse,* pp. 40, 50 f. ; Volkmar, *Der Ursprung,* p. 52 ; *Handbuch Einl. Apocr.* i. pp. 121 f., 136.

" ' [4] Volkmar, *Handbuch Einl. Apocr.* i. pp. 121 ff., 136 f. ; *Der Ursprung,* p. 52 ff. ; Baur, *Ursp. d. Episc., Tüb. Zeitschr. f. Theol.*

---

[1] "A Few Words on 'S. R.,'" preface to *Hist. of Canon,* 4th ed. p. xix f.
[2] *S. R.* i. p. 263.

1838, H. 3, p. 149 f. ; *Gesch. chr. Kirche*, 1863, i. p. 440, Anm. 1 ; Davidson, *Introd. N. T.* i. p. 19 ; Scholten, *Die ält. Zeugnisse*, p. 51 f. ; cf. Francke, *Zur Gesch. Trajans u.s.w.* 1840, p. 253 f. ; Hilgenfeld, *Die ap. Väter*, p. 214.' "

Upon this Dr. Westcott remarks :—

"Such an array of authorities, drawn from different schools, cannot but appear overwhelming ; and the fact that about half of them are quoted twice over emphasises the implied precision of their testimony as to the two points affirmed." [1]

Dr. Westcott, however, has either overlooked or omitted to state the fact that, although some of the writers are quoted twice, the two notes differ in almost every particular, many of the names in note 3 being absent from note 4, other names being inserted in the latter which do not appear in the former, an alteration being in most cases made in the place referred to, and the order in which the authorities are placed being significantly varied. For instance, in note 3, the reference to Volkmar is the last, but it is the first in note 4 ; whilst a similar transposition of order takes place in his works, and alterations are made in the pages. The references in note 3, in fact, are given for the date occurring in the course of the sentence, whilst those in note 4, placed at the end, are intended to support the whole statement which is made. I must, however, explain an omission, which is pretty obvious, but which I regret may have misled Dr. Westcott in regard to note 3, although it does not affect note 4. Readers are probably aware that there has been, amongst other points, a difference of opinion not only as to the place, but also the date of the martyrdom of Ignatius. I have in every other case carefully stated the question of date, and my omission in this instance is, I think, the only exception in the book. The fact is, that I had originally in the text the words which I now

---

[1] *On the Canon*, Preface, 4th ed. p. xx.

add to the note : " The martyrdom has been variously dated about A.D. 107, or A.D. 115–116, but whether assigning the event to Rome or to Antioch a majority of critics of all shades of opinion have adopted the later date." Thinking it unnecessary, under the circumstances, to burden the text with this, I removed it with the design of putting the statement at the head of note 3, with reference to " A.D. 115 " in the text, but unfortunately an interruption at the time prevented the completion of this intention, as well as the addition of some fuller references to the writers quoted, which had been omitted, and the point, to my infinite regret, was overlooked. The whole of the authorities in note 3, therefore, do not support the apparent statement of martyrdom in Antioch, although they all confirm the date, for which I really referred to them. With this explanation, and marking the omitted references [1] by placing them within brackets, I proceed to analyse the two notes in contrast with Dr. Westcott's statements.

Note 3, for the Date a.d. 115–116.

Dr. Westcott's Statements.	The Truth.
	Baur, *Urspr. d. Episc.*, *Tüb. Zeitschr.* 1838, H. 3 (p. 149, Anm.)
	Baur states as the date of the Parthian war, and of Trajan's visit to Rome, "during which the above order" (the sentence against Ignatius) is said to have been given, A.D. 115 and not 107.
" 1. Baur, *Urspr. d. Episc.*, *Tüb. Zeitschr.* 1838, ii. 3. p. 155, Anm. In this note, which is too long to quote, *there is nothing*, so far as I see, *in any way bearing*	*Ibid.* p. 155, Anm. After showing the extreme improbability of the circumstances under which the letters to the Smyrnæans and to Poly-

---

[1] These consist only of an additional page of Baur's work first quoted, and a reference to another of his works quoted in the second note, but accidentally left out of note 3.

DR. WESTCOTT'S STATEMENTS.

upon the history[1] except a passing supposition ' wenn . . . Ignatius im J. 116 an ihn [Polycarp] . . . schrieb . . .'

THE TRUTH.

carp are said to have been written, Baur points out the additional difficulty in regard to the latter that, if Polycarp died in A.D. 167 in his 86th year, and Ignatius wrote to him as already Bishop of Smyrna in A.D. 116, he must have become bishop at least in his 35th year, and continued so for upwards of half a century. The inference is clear that if Ignatius died so much earlier as A.D. 107 it involves the still greater improbability that Polycarp must have become Bishop of Smyrna at latest in his 26th year, which is scarcely to be maintained, and the later date is thus obviously supported.

(Ibid. *Gesch. christl. Kirche*, i. p. 440, Anm. 1.)

Baur supports the assertion that Ignatius suffered martyrdom in Antioch, A.D. 115.

" 2. Bretschneider, *Probabilia*, x. p. 185. ' Pergamus ad Ignatium '*qui circa annum cxvi obiisse dicitur.*'

The same.

" 3. Bleek, *Einl. N. T.* p. 144 [p. 142 ed. 1862] '. . . In den Briefen des Ignatius Bischofes von Antiochien, der unter Trajan gegen 115 *zu Rom* als Märtyrer starb.'

Bleek, *Einl. N. T.* p. 144.

Ignatius suffered martyrdom at Rome under Trajan, A.D. 115.

" 4. Guericke, *Handb. K. G.* i. p. 148 [p. 177 ed. 3, 1838, the edition which I have used]. 'Ignatius, Bischoff von Antiochien (Euseb. "H. E." iii. 36), *welcher wegen seines standhaften Be-*

Guericke, *Handbuch K. G.* i. p. 148.

Ignatius was sent to Rome, under Trajan, A.D. 115, and was destroyed by lions in the Coliseum, A.D. 116.

---

[1] I take the liberty of putting these words in italics to call attention to the assertion opposed to what I find in the note.

DR. WESTCOTT'S STATEMENTS.	THE TRUTH.

kenntnisses Christi *unter Trajan* 115 *nach Rom geführt, und hier* 116 *im Colosseum von Löwen zerrissen wurde* (vgl. § 23, i.)' [where the same statement is repeated].

"5. Hagenbach, *K. G.* i. 113 f. [I have not been able to see the book referred to, but in his Lectures 'Die christliche Kirche der drei ersten Jahrhunderte,'[1] 1853 (pp. 122 ff.), Hagenbach mentions the difficulty which has been felt as to the execution at Rome, while an execution at Antioch might have been simpler and more impressive, and then quotes Gieseler's solution, and passes on with ' Wie dem auch sei.']

"6. Davidson, *Introd. N. T.* i. p. 19. 'All [the Epistles of Ignatius] are posterior to Ignatius himself, who was not thrown to the wild beasts in the amphitheatre at Rome by command of Trajan, but at Antioch on December 20, A.D. 115. The Epistles were written after 150 A.D.' [For these peremptory statements no authority whatever is adduced].

"7. Mayerhoff, *Einl. petr. Schr.* p. 79. '. . . Ignatius, *der spätestens* 117 *zu Rom den Märtyrertod litt.* . . .'

"8. Scholten, *Die ält. Zeug-*

Hagenbach, *K. G.* 1869, p. 113 f.

" He (Ignatius) may have filled his office about 40 years when the Emperor, in the year 115 (according to others still earlier), came to Antioch. It was during his war against the Parthians." [Hagenbach states some of the arguments for and against the martyrdom in Antioch, and the journey to Rome, the former of which he seems to consider more probable.]

Davidson, *Introd. N. T.* i. p. 19.

The same as opposite.

These " peremptory statements " are of course based upon what is considered satisfactory evidence, though it may not be adduced here.

Mayerhoff, *Einl. petr. Schr.* p. 79.

Ignatius suffered martyrdom in Rome at latest A.D. 117.

Scholten, *Die ält. Zeugnisse,*

---

[1] It is the same work, I believe, subsequently published in an extended form. The work I quote is entitled *Kirchengeschichte der ersten sechs Jahrhunderte,* dritte, umgearbeitete Auflage, 1869, and is part of a course of lectures carrying the history to the nineteenth century.

DR. WESTCOTT'S STATEMENTS.	THE TRUTH.
nisse, p. 40, mentions 115 as the year of Ignatius' death : p. 50 f. The Ignatian letters are rejected partly 'weil sie eine Märtyrerreise des Ignatius nach Rom melden, deren schon früher erkanntes ungeschichtliches Wesen durch Volkmar's nicht ungegründete Vermuthung um so wahrscheinlicher wird. Darnach scheint nämlich Ignatius nicht zu Rom auf Befehl des sanftmüthigen Trajans, sondern zu Antiochia selbst, in Folge eines am dreizehnten December 115 eingetretenen Erdbebens, als Opfer eines abergläubischen Volkswahns am zwanzigsten December dieses Jahres im Amphitheater den wilden Thieren zur Beute überliefert worden zu sein.'	p. 40, states A.D. 115 as the date of Ignatius' death. At p. 50 he repeats this statement, and gives his support to the view that his martyrdom took place in Antioch on the 20th December, A.D. 115.
"9. Volkmar, *Der Ursprung*, p. 52 [p. 52 ff.]¹ [This book I have not been able to consult, but from secondary references I gather that it repeats the arguments given under the next reference.]	Volkmar, *Der Ursprung*, p. 52, affirms the martyrdom at Antioch, 20th December, 115.
"10. Volkmar, *Handb. Einl. Apocr.* pp. 121 f., 136. 'Ein Haupt der Gemeinde zu Antiochia, Ignatius, wurde, während Trajan dortselbst überwinterte, am 20. December den Thieren vorgeworfen, in Folge der durch das Erdbeben vom 13. December 115 gegen die ἄθεοι erweck-	Ibid. *Handbuch Einl. Apocr.* p. 121 f., affirms the martyrdom at Antioch, 20th December, 115.

---

¹ I do not know why Dr. Westcott adds the 'ff' to my reference, but I presume it is taken from note 4, where the reference is given to 'p. 52 ff.' This shows how completely he has failed to see the different object of the two notes.

DR. WESTCOTT'S STATEMENTS.	THE TRUTH.
ten Volkswuth, ein Opfer zu-gleich der Siegesfeste des Parthi-cus, welche die Judith-Erzählung (i. 16) andeutet, Dio (c. 24 f. ; vgl. c. 10) voraussetzt . . .'	
"P. 136. The same state-ment is repeated briefly." [1]	Ibid. p. 136. The same state-ment, with fuller chronological evidence.

It will thus be seen that the whole of these authorities confirm the later date assigned to the martyrdom, and that Baur, in the note in which Dr. Westcott finds "nothing in any way bearing upon the history except a passing supposition," really advances a weighty argument for it and against the earlier date, and as Dr. Westcott considers, rightly, that argument should decide everything, I am surprised that he has not per-ceived the propriety of my referring to arguments as well as statements of evidence.

To sum up the opinions expressed, I may state that whilst all the nine writers support the later date, for which purpose they were quoted, three of them (Bleek, Guericke, and Mayerhoff) ascribe the martyrdom to Rome, one (Bretschneider) mentions no place, one (Hagenbach) is doubtful, but leans to Antioch, and the other four declare for the martyrdom in Antioch. Nothing, however, could show more conclusively the purpose of note 3, which I have explained, than this very contradiction, and the fact that I claim for the general statement in the text, regarding the martyrdom in Antioch itself in opposition to the legend of the journey to and death in Rome, only the authorities in note 4, which I shall now proceed to analyse in contrast with Dr. Westcott's statements, and here I beg the favour of the reader's attention.

---

[1] *On the Canon*, Pref. 4th ed. p. xxi f.

NOTE 4.

DR. WESTCOTT'S STATEMENTS.	THE TRUTH.

DR. WESTCOTT'S STATEMENTS.

1. Volkmar : see above.

THE TRUTH.

Volkmar, *Handbuch Einl. Apocr.* i. pp. 121 ff., 136 f.

It will be observed on turning to the passage "above" (10), to which Dr. Westcott refers, that he quotes a single sentence containing merely a concise statement of facts, and that no indication is given to the reader that there is anything beyond it. At p. 136 "the same statement is repeated briefly." Now either Dr. Westcott, whilst bringing a most serious charge against my work, based upon this "one example," has actually not taken the trouble to examine my reference to "pp. 121 ff., 136 f.," and p. 50 ff., to which he would have found himself there directed, or he has acted towards me with a want of fairness which I venture to say he will be the first to regret, when he considers the facts.

Would it be divined from the words opposite, and the sentence "above," that Volkmar enters into an elaborate argument, extending over a dozen closely printed pages, to prove that Ignatius was not sent to Rome at all, but suffered martyrdom in Antioch itself on the 20th December, A.D. 115, probably as a sacrifice to the superstitious fury of the people against the ἄθεοι, excited by the earthquake which occurred on the thirteenth of that month? I shall not here

| DR. WESTCOTT'S STATEMENTS. | THE TRUTH. |

attempt to give even an epitome of the reasoning, as I shall presently reproduce some of the arguments of Volkmar and others in a more condensed and consecutive form.

· Ibid. *Der Ursprung*, p. 52 ff.

Volkmar repeats the affirmations which he had fully argued in the above work and elsewhere.

Baur, *Urspr. d. Episc., Tüb. Zeitschr.* 1838, H. 3, p. 149 f.

2. "Baur, *Ursprung d. Episc., Tüb. Zeitschr.* 1838, ii. H. 3, p. 149 f.

"In this passage Baur discusses generally the historical character of the martyrdom, which he considers, as a whole, to be 'doubtful and incredible.' To establish this result he notices the relation of Christianity to the Empire in the time of Trajan, which he regards as inconsistent with the condemnation of Ignatius; and the improbable circumstances of the journey. The personal characteristics, the letters, the history of Ignatius, are, in his opinion, all a mere creation of the imagination. The utmost he allows is that he may have suffered martyrdom." (P. 169.)

Baur enters into a long and minute examination of the historical character of the martyrdom of Ignatius, and of the Ignatian Epistles, and pronounces the whole to be fabulous, and more especially the representation of his sentence and martyr-journey to Rome. He shows that, while isolated cases of condemnation to death, under certain circumstances, which occurred during Trajan's reign may justify the mere tradition that he suffered martyrdom, there is no instance recorded in which a Christian was condemned to be sent to Rome to be cast to the beasts; that such a sentence is opposed to all historical data of the reign of Trajan, and to all that is known of his character and principles; and that the whole of the statements regarding the supposed journey directly discredit the story. The argument is much too long and elaborate to reproduce here, but I shall presently make use of some parts of it.

DR. WESTCOTT'S STATEMENTS.

3. "Baur, *Gesch. chr: Kirche,* 1863, i. p. 440, Anm. 1.

"'Die Verurtheilung *ad bestias* und die Abführung dazu nach Rom . . . mag auch unter Trajan nichts zu ungewöhnliches gewesen sein, aber . . bleibt die Geschichte seines Märtyrerthums auch nach der Vertheidigung derselben von Lipsius . . . höchst unwahrscheinlich. Das Factische ist wohl nur dass Ignatius im J. 115, als Trajan in Antiochien überwinterte, in Folge des Erdbebens in diesem Jahr, in Antiochien selbst als ein Opfer der Volkswuth zum Märtyrer wurde.'"

4. Davidson : see above.

5. Scholten : see above.

THE TRUTH.

Ibid., *Gesch. chr. Kirche,* 1863, i. p. 440, Anm. 1.

"The reality is 'wohl nur' that in the year 115, when Trajan wintered in Antioch, Ignatius suffered martyrdom in Antioch itself, as a sacrifice to popular fury consequent on the earthquake of that year. The rest was developed out of the reference to Trajan for the glorification of martyrdom."

Davidson, *Introd. N. T.,* i. p. 19.

"All (the Epistles) are posterior to Ignatius himself, who was not thrown to the wild beasts in the amphitheatre at Rome by command of Trajan, but at Antioch, on December 20th, A.D. 115.

Scholten, *Die ält. Zeugnisse,* p. 51 f.

The Ignatian Epistles are declared to be spurious for various reasons, but partly "because they mention a martyr-journey of Ignatius to Rome, the unhistorical character of which, already earlier recognised (see Baur, *Urspr. des Episc.* 1838, p. 147 ff., *Die Ign. Briefe,* 1848; Schwegler, *Nachap. Zeitalt.* ii. p. 159 ff.; Hilgenfeld, *Apost. Väter,* p. 210 ff.; Réville, *Le Lien,* 1856, Nos. 18–22), is made all the more probable by Volkmar's not groundless con-

DR. WESTCOTT'S STATEMENTS.	THE TRUTH.

THE TRUTH (right column continuation):

jecture. According to it Ignatius is reported to have become the prey of wild beasts on the 20th December, 115, not in the amphitheatre in Rome by the order of the mild Trajan, but in Antioch itself, as the victim of superstitious popular fury consequent on an earthquake which occurred on the 13th December of that year."

6. "Francke, *Zur Gesch. Trajan's*, 1840 [1837], p. 253 f. [A discussion of the date of the beginning of Trajan's Parthian war, which he fixes in A.D. 115, but he decides nothing directly as to the time of Ignatius' martyrdom.]"

Cf. Francke, *Zur Gesch. Trajan's*, 1840. This is a mere comparative reference to establish the important point of the date of the Parthian war and Trajan's visit to Antioch. Dr. Westcott omits the " Cf."

7. "Hilgenfeld, *Die ap. Väter*, p. 214 [pp. 210 ff.] Hilgenfeld points out the objections to the narrative in the Acts of the Martyrdom, the origin of which he refers to the period between Eusebius and Jerome : setting aside this detailed narrative he considers the historical character of the general statements in the letters. The mode of punishment by a provincial governor causes some difficulty : 'bedenklicher,' he continues, 'ist jedenfalls der andre Punct, die Versendung nach Rom.' Why was the punishment not carried out at Antioch ? Would it be likely that under an Emperor like Trajan a prisoner like Ignatius

Hilgenfeld, *Die ap. Väter*, p. 214 ff. Hilgenfeld strongly supports Baur's argument which is referred to above, and while declaring the whole story of Ignatius, and more especially the journey to Rome, incredible, he considers the mere fact that Ignatius suffered martyrdom the only point regarding which the possibility has been made out. He shows [1] that the martyrology states the 20th December as the day of Ignatius' death, and that his remains were buried at Antioch, where they still were in the days of Chrysostom and Jerome. He argues from all that is known of the reign and character of Trajan, that such a sentence

[1] P. 213.

DR. WESTCOTT'S STATEMENTS.	THE TRUTH.
would be sent to Rome to fight in the amphitheatre? The circumstances of the journey as described are most improbable. The account of the persecution itself is beset by difficulties. Having set out these objections he leaves the question, casting doubt (like Baur) upon the whole history, and gives no support to the bold affirmation of a martyrdom 'at Antioch on the 20th December, A.D. 115.' "	from the Emperor himself is quite unsupported and inconceivable. A provincial Governor might have condemned him *ad bestias*, but in any case the transmission to Rome is more doubtful. He shows, however, that the whole story is inconsistent with historical facts, and the circumstances of the journey incredible. It is impossible to give even a sketch of this argument, which extends over five long pages, but although Hilgenfeld does not directly refer to the theory of the martyrdom in Antioch itself, his reasoning forcibly points to that conclusion, and forms part of the converging trains of reasoning which result in that "demonstration" which I assert. I will presently make use of some of his arguments.

At the close of this analysis Dr. Westcott sums up the result as follows :—

"In this case, therefore, again, Volkmar alone offers any arguments in support of the statement in the text ; and the final result of the references is, that the alleged 'demonstration' is, at the most, what Scholten calls 'a not groundless conjecture.' " [1]

It is scarcely possible to imagine a more complete misrepresentation of the fact than the assertion that " Volkmar alone offers any arguments in support of the statement in the text," and it is incomprehensible upon any ordinary theory. My mere sketch cannot possibly

---

[1] *On the Canon*, Preface, 4th ed. p. xxiv. Dr. Westcott adds, in a note, "It may be worth while to add that in spite of the profuse display of learning in connection with Ignatius, I do not see even in the second edition any reference to the full and elaborate work of Zahn." I might reply to this that my MS. had left my hands before Zahn's work had reached England, but, moreover, the work contains nothing new to which reference was necessary.

convey an adequate idea of the elaborate arguments of Volkmar, Baur, and Hilgenfeld, but I hope to state their main features, a few pages on. With regard to Dr. Westcott's remark on the "alleged 'demonstration,'" it must be evident that when a writer states anything to be "demonstrated" he expresses his own belief. It is impossible to secure absolute unanimity of opinion, and the only question in such a case is whether I refer to writers, in connection with the circumstances which I affirm to be demonstrated, who advance arguments and evidence bearing upon it. A critic is quite at liberty to say that the arguments are insufficient, but he is not at liberty to deny that there are any arguments at all when the elaborate reasoning of men like Volkmar, Baur, and Hilgenfeld is referred to. Therefore, when he goes on to say :—

"It seems quite needless to multiply comments on these results. Anyone who will candidly consider this analysis will, I believe, agree with me in thinking that such a style of annotation, which runs through the whole work, is justly characterised as frivolous and misleading "— [1]

Dr. Westcott must excuse my retorting that, not my annotation, but his own criticism of it, endorsed by Professor Lightfoot, is "frivolous and misleading," and I venture to hope that this analysis, tedious as it has been, may once for all establish the propriety and substantial accuracy of my references.

As Dr. Westcott does not advance any further arguments of his own in regard to the Ignatian controversy, I may now return to Dr. Lightfoot, and complete my reply to his objections ; but I must do so with extreme brevity, as I have already devoted too much space to this subject, and must now come to a close. To the argument that it is impossible to suppose that soldiers

___
[1] *On the Canon*, Preface, 4th ed. p. xxv.

such as the " ten leopards " described in the Epistles
would allow a prisoner, condemned to wild beasts for
professing Christianity, deliberately to write long epistles
at every stage of his journey, promulgating the very
doctrines for which he was condemned, as well as to
hold the freest intercourse with deputations from the
various Churches, Dr. Lightfoot advances arguments,
derived from Zahn, regarding the Roman procedure in
cases that are said to be " known."   These cases, however, are neither analogous, nor have they the force
which is assumed.   That Christians imprisoned for their
religious belief should receive their nourishment, while
in prison, from friends, is anything but extraordinary,
and that bribes should secure access to them in many
cases, and some mitigation of suffering, is possible.
The case of Ignatius, however, is very different.   If the
meaning of οἳ καὶ εὐεργετούμενοι χείρους γίνονται be
that, although receiving bribes, the " ten leopards "
only became more cruel, the very reverse of the
leniency and mild treatment ascribed to the Roman
procedure is described by the writer himself as actually
taking place, and certainly nothing approaching a
parallel to the correspondence of pseudo-Ignatius can
be pointed out in any known instance.   The case of
Saturus and Perpetua, even if true, is no confirmation,
the circumstances being very different;[1] but in fact
there is no evidence whatever that the extant history
was written by either of them,[2] but on the contrary, I
maintain, every reason to believe that it was not.

Dr. Lightfoot advances the instance of Paul as a
case in point of a Christian prisoner treated with great
consideration, and who " writes letters freely, receives

---

[1] Ruinart, *Acta Mart.* p. 137 ff.; cf. Baronius, *Mart. Rom.* 1031, p.
152.
[2] Cf. Lardner, *Credibility,* &c., *Works,* iii. p. 3.

visits from his friends, communicates with Churches and individuals as he desires."[1] It is scarcely possible to imagine two cases more dissimilar than those of pseudo-Ignatius and Paul, as narrated in the " Acts of the Apostles," although doubtless the story of the former has been framed upon some of the lines of the latter. Whilst Ignatius is condemned to be cast to the wild beasts as a Christian, Paul is not condemned at all, but stands in the position of a Roman citizen, rescued from infuriated Jews (xxiii. 27), repeatedly declared by his judges to have done nothing worthy of death or of bonds (xxv. 25, xxvi. 31), and who might have been set at liberty but that he had appealed to Cæsar (xxv. 11 f., xxvi. 32). His position was one which secured the sympathy of the Roman soldiers. Ignatius " fights with beasts from Syria even unto Rome," and is cruelly treated by his " ten leopards," but Paul is represented as receiving very different treatment. Felix commands that his own people should be allowed to come and minister to him (xxiv. 23), and when the voyage is commenced it is said that Julius, who had charge of Paul, treated him courteously, and gave him liberty to go to see his friends at Sidon (xxvii. 3). At Rome he was allowed to live by himself with a single soldier to guard him (xxviii. 16), and he continued for two years in his own hired house (xxviii. 28). These circumstances are totally different from those under which the Epistles of Ignatius are said to have been written.

"But the most powerful testimony," Dr. Lightfoot goes on to say, " is derived from the representations of a heathen writer."[2] The case of Peregrinus, to which he refers, seems to me even more unfortunate than that of Paul. Of Peregrinus himself, historically, we really

---

[1] *Contemporary Review*, February 1875, p. 349 [*ibid*. p. 75].
[2] *Ibid*. p. 350 [*ibid*. p. 76].

know little or nothing, for the account of Lucian is scarcely received as serious by anyone.[1]   Lucian narrates that this Peregrinus Proteus, a cynic philosopher, having been guilty of parricide and other crimes, found it convenient to leave his own country.   In the course of his travels he fell in with Christians and learnt their doctrines, and, according to Lucian, the Christians soon were mere children in his hands, so that he became in his own person "prophet, high-priest, and ruler of a synagogue," and further "they spoke of him as a god, used him as a lawgiver, and elected him their chief man."[2]   After a time he was put in prison for his new faith, which Lucian says was a real service to him afterwards in his impostures.   During the time he was in prison he is said to have received those services from Christians which Dr. Lightfoot quotes.   Peregrinus was afterwards set at liberty by the Governor of Syria, who loved philosophy,[3] and travelled about, living in great comfort at the expense of the Christians, until at last they quarrelled in consequence, Lucian thinks, of his eating some forbidden food.   Finally, Peregrinus ended his career by throwing himself into the flames of a funeral pile during the Olympian games.   An earthquake is said to have taken place at the time; a vulture flew out from the pile crying out with a human voice; and, shortly after, Peregrinus rose again and appeared clothed in white raiment, unhurt by the fire.

Now this writing, of which I have given the barest sketch, is a direct satire upon Christians, or even, as Baur affirms, "a parody of the history of Jesus."[4] There are no means of ascertaining that any of the events of the Christian career of Peregrinus were true,

---

[1] There are grave reasons for considering it altogether inauthentic.   Cf. Cotterill, *Peregrinus Proteus*, 1870.   [2] *De Morte Peregr.* 11.
[3] *Ibid.* 14.   [4] *Gesch. chr. Kirche*, i. p. 410 f.

but it is obvious that Lucian's policy was to exaggerate
the facility of access to prisoners, as well as the assiduity
and attention of the Christians to Peregrinus, the ease
with which they were duped being the chief point of
the satire.

There is another circumstance which must be mentioned. Lucian's account of Peregrinus is claimed by
supporters of the Ignatian Epistles as evidence for
them.[1]   " The singular correspondence in this narrative
with the account of Ignatius, combined with some
striking coincidences of expression," they argue, show
" that Lucian was acquainted with the Ignatian history,
if not with the Ignatian letters."   These are the words
of Dr. Lightfoot, although he guards himself, in referring
to this argument, by the words " if it be true," and
does not express his own opinion; but he goes on to
say : " At all events it is conclusive for the matter in
hand, as showing that Christian prisoners were treated
in the very way described in these epistles."[2]   On the
contrary, it is in no case conclusive of anything.   If it
were true that Lucian employed, as the basis of his
satire, the Ignatian Epistles and Martyrology, it is clear
that his narrative cannot be used as independent testimony for the truth of the statements regarding the
treatment of Christian prisoners.   On the other hand,
as this cannot be shown, his story remains a mere satire
with very little historical value.   Apart from all this,
however, the case of Peregrinus, a man confined in
prison for a short time, under a favourable governor,
and not pursued with any severity, is no parallel to that
of Ignatius condemned *ad bestias* and, according to his
own express statement, cruelly treated by the " ten
leopards ; " and further the liberty of pseudo-Ignatius

[1] See, for instance, Denzinger, *Ueber die Aechtheit d. bish. Textes d. Ignat.
Briefe*, 1849, p. 87 ff.; Zahn, *Ignatius v. Ant.* 1873, p. 517 ff.
[2] *Contemporary Review*, February 1875, p. 350 f. [*ibid.* p. 77].

must greatly have exceeded all that is said of Peregrinus, if he was able to write such epistles, and hold
such free intercourse as they represent.

I will now, in the briefest manner possible, indicate
the arguments of the writers referred to in the note [1]
attacked by Dr. Westcott, in which he cannot find any
relevancy, but which, in my opinion, demonstrate that
Ignatius was not sent to Rome at all, but suffered
martyrdom in Antioch itself. The reader who wishes
to go minutely into the matter must be good enough to
consult the writers there cited, and I will only sketch
the case here, without specifically indicating the source
of each argument. Where I add any particulars I will,
when necessary, give my authorities. The Ignatian
Epistles and martyrologies set forth that, during a
general persecution of Christians, in Syria at least,
Ignatius was condemned by Trajan, when he wintered
in Antioch during the Parthian War, to be taken to
Rome and cast to wild beasts in the amphitheatre.
Instead of being sent to Rome by the short sea voyage,
he is represented as taken thither by the long and in-
comparably more difficult land route. The ten soldiers
who guard him are described by himself as only rendered more cruel by the presents made to them to
secure kind treatment for him, so that not in the
amphitheatre only, but all the way from Syria to Rome,
by night and day, by sea and land, he "fights with
beasts." Notwithstanding this severity, the martyr
freely receives deputations from the various Churches,
who, far from being molested, are able to have constant
intercourse with him, and even to accompany him on
his journey. He not only converses with these freely,
but he is represented as writing long epistles to the
various Churches, which, instead of containing the last

[1] *S. R.* i. p. 268, note 4.

exhortations and farewell words which might be considered natural from the expectant martyr, are filled
with advanced views of Church government, and the
dignity of the episcopate. These circumstances, at the
outset, excite grave suspicions of the truth of the
documents and of the story which they set forth.

When we enquire whether the alleged facts of the
case are supported by historical data, the reply is emphatically adverse. All that is known of the treatment
of Christians during the reign of Trajan, as well as of
the character of the Emperor, is opposed to the supposition that Ignatius could have been condémned by
Trajan himself, or even by a provincial governor, to be
taken to Rome and there cast to the beasts. It is well
known that under Trajan there was no general persecution of Christians, although there may have been instances in which prominent members of the body were
either punished or fell victims to popular fury and
superstition.[1] An instance of this kind was the martyrdom of Simeon, Bishop of Jerusalem, reported by Hegesippus. He was not condemned *ad bestias*, however,
and much less deported to Rome for the purpose. Why
should Ignatius have been so exceptionally treated?
In fact, even during the persecutions under Marcus
Aurelius, although Christians in Syria were frequently
enough cast to the beasts, there is no instance recorded
in which anyone condemned to this fate was sent to
Rome. Such a sentence is quite at variance with the
clement character of Trajan and his principles of government. Neander, in a passage quoted by Baur, says :
" As he (Trajan), like Pliny, considered Christianity

---

[1] Dean Milman says: " Trajan, indeed, is absolved, at least by the almost
general voice of antiquity, from the crime of persecuting the Christians."
In a note he adds : " Excepting of Ignatius, probably of Simeon of Jerusalem, there is no authentic martyrdom in the reign of Trajan."—*Hist. of
Christianity*, 1867, ii. p. 103.

mere fanaticism, he also probably thought that if severity were combined with clemency, if too much noise were not made about it, the open demonstration not left unpunished but also minds not stirred up by persecution, the fanatical enthusiasm would most easily cool down, and the matter by degrees come to an end."[1] This was certainly the policy which mainly characterised his reign. Now not only would this severe sentence have been contrary to such principles, but the agitation excited would have been enormously increased by sending the martyr a long journey by land through Asia, and allowing him to pass through some of the principal cities, hold constant intercourse with the various Christian communities, and address long epistles to them. With the fervid desire for martyrdom then prevalent, such a journey would have been a triumphal progress, spreading everywhere excitement and enthusiasm. It may not be out of place, as an indication of the results of impartial examination, to point out that Neander's inability to accept the Ignatian Epistles largely rests on his disbelief of the whole tradition of this sentence and martyr-journey. "We do not recognise the Emperor Trajan in this narrative" (the martyrology), he says, " therefore cannot but doubt everything which is related by this document, as well as that, during this reign, Christians can have been cast to the wild beasts."[2]

If, for a moment, we suppose that, instead of being condemned by Trajan himself, Ignatius received his sentence from a provincial governor, the story does not gain greater probability. It is not credible that such an official would have ventured to act so much in opposition to the spirit of the Emperor's government. Besides, if such a governor did pronounce so severe a

---

[1] *K. G.* 1842, i. p. 171. [2] *Ibid.* i. p. 172, Anm.

sentence, why did he not execute it in Antioch? Why send the prisoner to Rome? By doing so he made all the more conspicuous a severity which was not likely to be pleasing to the clement Trajan. The cruelty which dictated a condemnation *ad bestias* would have been more gratified by execution on the spot, and there is besides no instance known, even during the following general persecution, of Christians being sent for execution in Rome. The transport to Rome is in no case credible, and the utmost that can be admitted is, that Ignatius, like Simeon of Jerusalem, may have been condemned to death during this reign, more especially if the event be associated with some sudden outbreak of superstitious fury against the Christians, to which the martyr may at once have fallen a victim. We are not without indications of such a cause operating in the case of Ignatius.

It is generally admitted that the date of Trajan's visit to Antioch is A.D. 115, when he wintered there during the Parthian War. An earthquake occurred on the 13th December of that year, which was well calculated to excite popular superstition. It may not be out of place to quote here the account of the earthquake given by Dean Milman, who, although he mentions a different date, and adheres to the martyrdom in Rome, still associates the condemnation of Ignatius with the earthquake. He says: "Nevertheless, at that time there were circumstances which account with singular likelihood for that sudden outburst of persecution in Antioch. . . . At this very time an earthquake, more than usually terrible and destructive, shook the cities of the East. Antioch suffered its most appalling ravages —Antioch, crowded with the legionaries prepared for the Emperor's invasion of the East, with ambassadors and tributary kings from all parts of the East. The city shook through all its streets; houses, palaces, theatres, temples fell crashing down. Many were killed: the Consul Pedo died of his hurts. The Emperor himself hardly escaped through a window, and took refuge in the Circus, where he passed some days in the open air. Whence this terrible blow.but from the wrath of the Gods, who must be appeased by unusual sacrifices? This was towards the end of January; early in February the Christian Bishop, Ignatius, was arrested. We know how, during this century, at every period of public calamity, whatever that calamity might be, the cry of the panic-stricken Heathens was, 'The Christians to the lions!' It may be that, in Trajan's humanity, in order to prevent a general massacre by the infuriated populace, or to give greater solemnity to the sacrifice, the execution was ordered to take place, not in Antioch, but in Rome." [1] I contend that these reasons, on the contrary, render execution in Antioch infinitely more probable. To continue, however: the earthquake occurred on the 13th, and the martyrdom of Ignatius took place on the 20th December, just a week after the earthquake. His remains, as we know from Chrysostom and others, were, as an actual fact, interred at Antioch. The natural inference is that the martyrdom, the only part of the Ignatian story which is credible, occurred not in Rome but in Antioch itself, in consequence of the superstitious fury against the $ἄθεοι$ aroused by the earthquake.

I will now go more into the details of the brief statements I have just made, and here we come for the first time to John Malalas. In the first place he mentions the occurrence of the earthquake on the 13th December. I will quote Dr. Lightfoot's own rendering of his further important statement. He says :—

---

[1] *Hist. of Christianity,* ii. p. 101 f.

"The words of John Malalas are: The same king Trajan was residing in the same city (Antioch) when the visitation of God (*i.e.* the earthquake) occurred. And at that time the holy Ignatius, the bishop of the city of Antioch, was martyred (or bore testimony, ἐμαρτύρησε) before him (ἐπὶ αὐτοῦ); for he was exasperated against him, because he reviled him.'" [1]

Dr. Lightfoot endeavours in every way to discredit this statement. He argues that Malalas tells foolish stories about other matters, and, therefore, is not to be believed here; but so simple a piece of information may well be correctly conveyed by a writer who elsewhere may record stupid traditions.[2] If the narrative of foolish stories and fabulous traditions is to exclude belief in everything else stated by those who relate them, the whole of the Fathers are disposed of at one fell swoop, for they all do so. Dr. Lightfoot also asserts that the theory of the cause of the martyrdom advanced by Volkmar "receives no countenance from the story of Malalas, who gives a wholly different reason—the irritating language used to the Emperor."[3] On the other hand, it in no way contradicts it, for Ignatius can only have "reviled" Trajan when brought before him, and his being taken before him may well have been caused by the fury excited by the earthquake, even if the language of the Bishop influenced his condemnation; the whole statement of Malalas is in perfect harmony with the theory in its details, and in the main, of course, directly supports it. Then Dr. Lightfoot actually makes use of the following extraordinary argument:—

"But it may be worth while adding that the error of Malalas is capable of easy explanation. He has probably misinterpreted some earlier authority, whose language lent itself to misinterpretation. The words μαρτυρεῖν, μαρτυρία, which were afterwards used especially

---

[1] P. 276 (ed. Bonn). *Contemporary Review*, February 1875, p. 352 [*ibid.* p. 79]. [2] *Ibid.* p. 353 f. [*ibid.* p. 80]. [3] *Ibid.* p. 352 [*ibid.* p. 79 f.].

of martyrdom, had in the earlier ages a wider sense, including other modes of witnessing to the faith : the expression ἐπὶ Τραϊανοῦ again is ambiguous and might denote either ' during the reign of Trajan,' or ' in the presence of Trajan.' A blundering writer like Malalas might have stumbled over either expression." [1]

This is a favourite device. In case his abuse of poor Malalas should not sufficiently discredit him, Dr. Lightfoot attempts to explain away his language. It would be difficult indeed to show that the words μαρτυρεῖν, μαρτυρία, already used in that sense in the New Testament, were not, at the date at which any record of the martyrdom of Ignatius which Malalas could have had before him was written, employed to express martyrdom, when applied to such a case, as Dr. Lightfoot indeed has in the first instance rendered the phrase. Even Zahn, whom Dr. Lightfoot so implicitly follows, emphatically decides against him on both points. "The ἐπὶ αὐτοῦ together with τότε can only signify ' coram Trajano' (' in the presence of Trajan '), and ἐμαρτύρησε only the execution." [2] Let anyone simply read over Dr. Lightfoot's own rendering, which I have quoted above, and he will see that such quibbles are excluded, and that, on the contrary, Malalas seems excellently well and directly to have interpreted his earlier authority.

That the statement of Malalas does not agree with the reports of the Fathers is no real objection, for we have good reason to believe that none of them had information from any other source than the Ignatian Epistles themselves, or tradition. Eusebius evidently had not. Irenæus, Origen, and some later Fathers tell us nothing about him. Jerome and Chrysostom clearly take their accounts from these sources. Malalas is the first who, by his variation, proves that he had another

---

[1] *Contemporary Review*, February 1875, p. 353 f. [*ibid.* p. 81].
[2] *Ignatius v. Ant.* p. 66, Anm. 3.

and different authority before him, and in abandoning the martyr-journey to Rome, his account has infinitely greater apparent probability. Malalas lived at Antioch, which adds some weight to his statement. It is objected that so also did Chrysostom, and at an earlier period, and yet he repeats the Roman story. This, however, is no valid argument against Malalas. Chrysostom was too good a churchman to doubt the story of Epistles so much tending to edification, which were in wide circulation, and had been quoted by earlier Fathers. It is in no way surprising that, some two centuries and a half after the martyrdom, he should quietly have accepted the representations of the Epistles purporting to have been written by the martyr himself, and that their story should have shaped the prevailing tradition.

The remains of Ignatius, as we are informed by Chrysostom and Jerome, long remained interred in the cemetery of Antioch, but finally—in the time of Theodosius, it is said—were translated with great pomp and ceremony to a building which—such is the irony of events—had previously been a Temple of Fortune. The story told, of course, is that the relics of the martyr had been carefully collected in the Coliseum and carried from Rome to Antioch. After reposing there for some centuries, the relics, which are said to have been transported from Rome to Antioch, were, about the seventh century, carried back from Antioch to Rome.[1] The natural and more simple conclusion is that, instead of this double translation, the bones of Ignatius had always remained in Antioch, where he had suffered martyrdom, and the tradition that they had been brought back from

---

[1] I need not refer to the statement of Nicephorus that these relics were first brought from Rome to Constantinople and afterwards translated to Antioch.

Rome was merely the explanation which reconciled the fact of their actually being in Antioch with the legend of the Ignatian Epistles.

The 20th of December is the date assigned to the death of Ignatius in the Martyrology,[1] and Zahn admits that this interpretation is undeniable.[2] Moreover, the anniversary of his death was celebrated on that day in the Greek Churches and throughout the East. In the Latin Church it is kept on the 1st of February. There can be little doubt that this was the day of the translation of the relics to Rome, and this was evidently the view of Ruinart, who, although he could not positively contradict the views of his own Church, says : " Ignatii festum Graeci vigesima die mensis Decembris celebrant, quo ipsum passum fuisse Acta testantur; Latini vero die prima Februarii, an ob aliquam sacrarum ejus reliquiarum translationem ? plures enim fuisse constat." [3] Zahn[4] states that the Feast of the translation in later calendars was celebrated on the 29th January, and he points out the evident ignorance which prevailed in the West regarding Ignatius.[5]

On the one hand, therefore, all the historical data which we possess regarding the reign and character of Trajan discredit the story that Ignatius was sent to Rome to be exposed to beasts in the Coliseum ; and all the positive evidence which exists, independent of the Epistles themselves, tends to establish the fact that he suffered martyrdom in Antioch. On the other hand,

[1] Ruinart, *Acta Mart.* pp. 59, 69.   [2] *Ignatius v. Ant.* p. 68.
[3] Ruinart, *Acta Mart.* p. 56. Baronius makes the anniversary of the martyrdom 1st February, and that of the translation 17th December. (*Mart. Rom.* pp. 87, 766 ff.)
[4] *Ignatius v. Ant.* p. 27, p. 68, Anm. 2.
[5] There is no sufficient evidence for the statement that, in Chrysostom's time, the day dedicated to Ignatius was in June. The mere allusion, in a Homily delivered in honour of Ignatius, that " recently " the feast of Sta. Pelagia (in the Latin Calendar 9th June) had been celebrated, by no means justifies such a conclusion, and there is nothing else to establish it.

all the evidence which is offered for the statement that Ignatius was sent to Rome is more or less directly based upon the representations of the letters, the authenticity of which is in discussion, and it is surrounded with improbabilities of every kind. And what is the value of any evidence emanating from the Ignatian Epistles and martyrologies? There are three martyrologies which, as Ewald says, are "the one more fabulous than the other." There are fifteen Epistles all equally purporting to be by Ignatius, and most of them handed down together in MSS., without any distinction. Three of these, in Latin only, are universally rejected, as are also other five Epistles, of which there are Greek, Latin, and other versions. Of the remaining seven there are two forms, one called the Long Recension and another shorter, known as the Vossian Epistles. The former is almost unanimously rejected as shamefully interpolated and falsified; and a majority of critics assert that the text of the Vossian Epistles is likewise very impure. Besides these there is a still shorter version of three Epistles only, the Curetonian, which many able critics declare to be the only genuine letters of Ignatius, whilst a still greater number, both from internal and external reasons, deny the authenticity of the Epistles in any form. The second and third centuries teem with pseudonymic literature, but I venture to say that pious fraud has never been more busy and conspicuous than in dealing with the Martyr of Antioch. The mere statement of the simple and acknowledged facts regarding the Ignatian Epistles is ample justification of the assertion, which so mightily offends Dr. Lightfoot, that "the whole of the Ignatian literature is a mass of falsification and fraud." Even my indignant critic himself has not ventured to use as genuine more than the three short

I

Syriac letters [1] out of this mass of forgery, which he
rebukes me for holding so cheap. Documents which
lie under such grave and permanent suspicion cannot
prove anything. As I have shown, however, the Vossian Epistles, whatever the value of their testimony, so
far from supporting the claims advanced in favour of
our Gospels, rather discredit them.

I have now minutely followed Dr. Lightfoot and
Dr. Westcott in their attacks upon me in connection
with Eusebius and the Ignatian Epistles, and I trust
that I have shown once for all that the charges of
" misrepresentation " and " misstatement," so lightly
and liberally advanced, far from being well-founded,
recoil upon themselves. It is impossible in a work like
this, dealing with such voluminous materials, to escape
errors of detail, as both of these gentlemen bear witness,
but I have at least conscientiously endeavoured to be
fair, and I venture to think that few writers have ever
more fully laid before readers the actual means of
judging of the accuracy of every statement which has
been made.

---

[1] *St. Paul's Ep. to the Philippians*, 3rd ed. 1873, p. 232, note. Cf. *Contemporary Review*, February 1875, p. 358 f. (*Ibid.* p. 88.)

III.

POLYCARP OF SMYRNA.

IN my chapter on Polycarp I state the various opinions expressed by critics regarding the authenticity of the Epistle ascribed to him, and I more particularly point out the reasons which have led many to decide that it is either spurious or interpolated.

That an Epistle of Polycarp did really exist at one time no one doubts, but the proof that the Epistle which is now extant was the actual Epistle written by Polycarp is not proven. Dr. Lightfoot's essay of course assumes the authenticity, and seeks to establish it. A large part of it is directed to the date which must be assigned to it on that supposition, and recent researches seem to establish that the martyrdom of Polycarp must be set some two years earlier than was formerly believed. The *Chronicon* of Eusebius dates his death A.D. 166 or 167, and he is said to have been martyred during the proconsulship of Statius Quadratus. M. Waddington, in examining the proconsular annals of Asia Minor, with the assistance of newly-discovered inscriptions, has decided that Statius Quadratus was proconsul in A.D. 154–155, and if Polycarp was martyred during his proconsulship it would follow that his death must have taken place in one of those years.

Having said so much in support of the authenticity

of the Epistle of Polycarp, and the earlier date to be assigned to it, it might have been expected that Dr. Lightfoot would have proceeded to show what bearing the epistle has upon the evidence for the existence of the Gospels and their sufficiency as testimony for the miracles which those Gospels record. He has not done so, however, for he is in such haste to find small faults with my statements, and disparage my work, that, having arrived at this point, he at once rushes off upon this side issue, and does not say one word that I can discover regarding any supposed use of Gospels in the Epistle. For a complete discussion of analogies which other apologists have pointed out I must refer to *Supernatural Religion* itself; [1] but I may here state the case in the strongest form for them. It is asserted that Polycarp in this Epistle uses expressions which correspond more or less closely with some of those in our Gospels. It is not in the least pretended that the Gospels are referred to by name, or that any information is given regarding their authorship or composition. If, therefore, the use of the Gospels could be established, and the absolute authenticity of the Epistle, what could this do towards proving the actual performance of miracles or the reality of Divine Revelation? The mere existence of anonymous Gospels would be indicated, and though this might be considered a good deal in the actual evidential destitution, it would leave the chief difficulty quite untouched.

---

[1] Complete ed. i. p. 277 f. All the references which I give in these essays must be understood as being to the complete edition.

IV.

PAPIAS OF HIERAPOLIS.

DR. LIGHTFOOT has devoted two long chapters to the evidence of Papias, although with a good deal of divergence to other topics in the second. I need not follow him minutely here, for I have treated the subject fully in *Supernàtural Religion*,[1] to which I beg leave to refer any reader who is interested in the discussion; and this is merely Dr. Lightfoot's reply. I will confine myself here to a few words on the fundamental question at issue.

Papias, in the absence of other testimony, is an important witness of whom theologians are naturally very tenacious, inasmuch as he is the first writer who mentions the name of anyone who was believed to have written a Gospel. It is true that what he says is of very little weight, but, since no one else had said anything at all on the point, his remarks merit attention which they would not otherwise receive.

Eusebius states that, in his last work, "Exposition of the Lord's Oracles" (Λογίων κυριακῶν ἐξήγησις), Papias wrote as follows :—

"And the elder said this also : 'Mark, having become the interpreter of Peter, wrote down accurately everything that he remembered, without, however, recording in order what was either said or

---

[1] i. p. 443 ff.

done by Christ. For neither did he hear the Lord, nor did he follow Him ; but afterwards, as I said, [attended] Peter, who adapted his instructions to the needs [of his hearers], but had no design of giving a connected account of the Lord's oracles [*or* discourses] (ἀλλ' οὐχ ὥσπερ σύνταξιν τῶν κυριακῶν ποιούμενος λογίων *or* λόγων).' So, then, Mark made no mistake while he thus wrote down some things as he remembered them ; for he made it his one care not to omit anything that he heard, or to set down any false statement therein." [1]

The first question which suggests itself is : Does the description here given corresponds with the Gospel " according to Mark " which we now possess ? Can our second Gospel be considered a work composed " without recording in order what was either said or done by Christ " ? A negative answer has been given by many eminent critics to these and similar enquiries, and the application of the Presbyter's words to it has consequently been denied by them. It does not follow from this that there has been any refusal to accept the words of Papias as referring to a work which may have been the basis of the second Gospel as we have it. However, I propose to waive all this objection, for the sake of argument, on the present occasion, and to consider what might be the value of the evidence before us, if it be taken as referring to our second Gospel.

In the first place, the tradition distinctly states that Mark, who is said to have been its author, was neither an eye-witness of the circumstances recorded, nor a hearer of the words of Jesus, but that he merely recorded what he remembered of the casual teaching of Peter. It is true that an assurance is added as to the general care and accuracy of Mark in recording all that he heard and not making any false statement, but this does not add much value to his record. No one supposes that the writer of the second Gospel deliberately invented what he has embodied in his work, and the

---

[1] This rendering is quoted from Dr. Lightfoot's *Essays*, p. 103.

certificate of character can be received for nothing more than a general estimate of the speaker. The testimony of the second Gospel is, according to this tradition, confessedly at second hand, and consequently utterly inadequate to attest miraculous pretensions. The tradition that Mark derived his information from the preaching of Peter is not supported by internal evidence, and has nothing extraneous to strengthen its probability. Because some person, whose very identity is far from established, says so, is not strong evidence of the fact. It was the earnest 'desire of the early Christians to connect Apostles with the authorship of the Gospels, and as Mark is represented as the interpreter of Peter, so Luke, or the third evangelist, is connected more or less closely with Paul, in forgetfulness of the circumstance that we have no reason whatever for believing that Paul ever saw Jesus. Comparison of the contents of the first three Gospels, moreover, not only does not render more probable this account of the composition of the second synoptic as it lies before us, but is really opposed to it. Into this I shall not here go.

Setting aside, therefore, all the reasons for doubting the applicability of the tradition recorded by Papias regarding the Gospel said to have been written by Mark, I simply appeal to those who have rightly appreciated the nature of the allegations for which evidence is required as to the value of such a work, compiled by one who had neither himself seen nor heard Jesus. It is quite unnecessary to proceed to the closer examination of the supposed evidence.

"But concerning Matthew the following statement is made [by Papias] : 'So then Matthew (Ματθαῖος μὲν οὖν) composed the Oracles in the Hebrew language, and each one interpreted them as he could.' " [1]

_____
[1] *Essays*, p. 167 f.

Dr. Lightfoot points out that there is no absolute reason for supposing that this statement, like the former, was made on the authority of the Presbyter, and, although I think it probable that it was, I agree with him in this. The doubt, however, is specially advanced because, the statement of Papias being particularly inconvenient to apologists, Dr. Lightfoot is evidently anxious to invalidate it. He accepts it in so far as it seems to permit of his drawing certain inferences from it, but for the rest he proceeds to weaken the testimony. "But it does not follow that his account of the origin was correct. It may be; it may not have been. This is just what we cannot decide, because we do not know what he said." [1] What a pity it is that Dr. Lightfoot does not always exercise this rigorous logic. If he did he would infallibly agree with the conclusions of *Supernatural Religion*. I shall presently state what inference Dr. Lightfoot wishes to draw from a statement the general correctness of which he does not consider as at all certain. If this doubt exist, however, of what value can the passage from Papias be as evidence?

I cannot perceive that, if we do not reject it altogether on the ground of possible or probable incorrectness, there can be any reasonable doubt as to what the actual statement was. "Matthew composed the Oracles in the Hebrew language," and not in Greek, "and each one interpreted them as he could." The original work of Matthew was written in Hebrew: our first synoptic is a Greek work: therefore it cannot possibly be the original composition of Matthew, whoever Matthew may have been, but at the best can only be a free translation. A free translation, I say, because it does not bear any of the traces of close translation. Our synoptic, indeed, does not purport to be a translation at all, but if it be

---

[1] *Essays*, p. 170.

a version of the work referred to by Papias, or the Presbyter, a translation it must be. As it is not in its original form, however, and no one can affirm what its precise relation to the work of Matthew may be, the whole value of the statement of Papias is lost.

The inference which Dr. Lightfoot considers himself entitled to draw from the testimony of Papias is in most curious contrast with his severe handling of that part of the testimony which does not suit him. Papias, or the Presbyter, states regarding the Hebrew Oracles of Matthew that " each one interpreted them as he could." The use of the verb " interpreted " in the past tense, instead of "interprets" in the present, he considers, clearly indicates that the time which Papias contemplates is not the time when he writes his book. Each one interpreted as he could when the Oracles were written, but the necessity of which he speaks had passed away; and Dr. Lightfoot arrives at the conclution : "In other words, it implies the existence of a recognised Greek translation *when Papias wrote.* . . . But if a Greek St. Matthew existed in the time of Papias, we are forbidden by all considerations of historical probability to suppose that it was any other than our St. Matthew." [1] It is very probable that, at the time when Papias wrote, there may have been several translations of the "Oracles" and not merely one, but from this to the assertion that the words imply a " recognised " version which was necessarily " our St. Matthew " is a remarkable jump at conclusions. It is really not worth while again to discuss the point. When imagination is allowed to interpret the hidden meaning of such a statement the consequence cannot well be predicated. This hypothesis still leaves us to account for the substitution of a Greek Gospel for the Hebrew original of Matthew,

[1] *Ibid.* p. 109.

and Dr. Lightfoot does not assist us much. He demurs to my statement that our first Gospel bears all the marks of an original, and cannot have been translated from the Hebrew at all : "If he had said that it is not a homogeneous Greek version of a homogeneous Hebrew original this would have been nearer the truth." [1]

That Hebrew original is a sad stumbling-block, and it must be got rid of at all costs. Dr. Lightfoot is full of resources. We have seen that he has suggested that the account of Papias of the origin may not have been correct. Regarding the translation or the Greek Gospel we do not know exactly what Papias said. "He may have expressed himself in language quite consistent with the phenomena." How unlimited a field for conjecture is thus opened out. We do not know more of what Papias said than Eusebius has recorded, and may therefore suppose that he may have said something more, which may have been consistent with any theory we may advance. "Or, on the other hand," Dr. Lightfoot continues, "he may, as Hilgenfeld supposes, have made the mistake which some later Fathers made of thinking that the Gospel according to the Hebrews was the original of our St. Matthew." [2] Who would think that this is the critic who vents so much righteous indignation upon me for pointing out possible or probable alternative interpretations of vague evidence extracted from the Fathers? It is true that Dr. Lightfoot continues : "In the absence of adequate data, it is quite vain to conjecture. But meanwhile we are not warranted in drawing any conclusion unfavourable either to the accuracy of Papias or to the identity of the document itself." [3] He thus seeks to reserve for himself any support he thinks he can derive from the tradition of Papias, and set aside exactly as much as he

[1] *Essays*, p. 170.   [2] *Ibid.* p. 170.   [3] *Ibid.* p. 170.

does not like. In fact, he clearly demonstrates how exceedingly loose is all this evidence from the Fathers, and with what ease one may either base magnificent conclusions upon it, or drive a coach and four through the whole mass.

In admitting for a moment that Papias may have mistaken the Gospel of the Hebrews "for the original of our St. Matthew," Dr. Lightfoot, in his attempt to get rid of that unfortunate Hebrew work of Matthew, has perhaps gone further than is safe for himself. Apart from the general flavour of inaccuracy which he imparts to the testimony of Papias, the obvious inference is suggested that, if he made this mistake, Papias is far from being a witness for the accuracy of the translation which Dr. Lightfoot supposes to have then been "recognised," and which he declares to have been our first Gospel. It is well known at least that, although the Gospel of the Hebrews bore more analogy to our present Gospel "according to Matthew" than to any of the other three, it very distinctly differed from it. If, therefore, Papias could quietly accept our Greek Matthew as an equivalent for the Gospel of the Hebrews, from which it presented considerable variation, we are entitled to reject such a translation as evidence of the contents of the original. That Papias was actually acquainted with the Gospel according to the Hebrews may be inferred from the statement of Eusebius that he relates "a story about a woman accused of many sins before the Lord" (doubtless the same which is found in our copies of St. John's Gospel, vii. 53–viii. 11), "which the Gospel according to the Hebrews contains." [1] If he exercised any critical power at all, he could not confound the Greek Matthew with it,

---

[1] *Ibid.* p. 152.

and if he did not, what becomes of Dr. Lightfoot's argument?

Dr. Lightfoot argues at considerable length against the interpretation, accepted by many eminent critics, that the work ascribed to Matthew and called the "Oracles" (λόγια) could not be the first synoptic as we now possess it, but must have consisted mainly or entirely of Discourses. The argument will be found in *Supernatural Religion*,[1] and need not here be repeated. I will confine myself to some points of Dr. Lightfoot's reply. He seems not to reject the suggestion with so much vigour as might have been expected. "The theory is not without its attractions," he says; "it promises a solution of some difficulties; but hitherto it has not yielded any results which would justify its acceptance." [2] Indeed, he proceeds to say that it "is encumbered with the most serious difficulties." Dr. Lightfoot does not think that only λόγοι ("discourses" or "sayings") could be called λόγια ("oracles"), and says that usage does not warrant the restriction.[3] I had contended that "however much the signification (of the expression 'the oracles,' τὰ λόγια) became afterwards extended, it was not then at all applied to doings as well as sayings," and that "there is no linguistic precedent for straining the expression, used at that period, to mean anything beyond a collection of sayings of Jesus, which were oracular or Divine." [4] To this Dr. Lightfoot replies that if the objection has any force it involves one or both of the two assumptions: "*first*, that books which were regarded as Scripture could not at this early date be called 'oracles,' unless they were occupied entirely with Divine sayings; *secondly*, that the Gospel of St. Matthew, in particular, could not at

---

[1] Vol. i. p. 463 f.   [2] *Ibid.* p. 171.
[3] *Ibid.* p. 172 f.   [4] i. p. 463 f.

this time be regarded as Scripture. Both assumptions alike are contradicted by facts." [1] The second point he considers proved by the well-known passage in the Epistle of Barnabas. For the discussion regarding it I beg leave to refer the reader to my volumes.[2] I venture to say that it is impossible to prove that Matthew's Gospel was, at that time, considered "Scripture," but, on the contrary, that there are excellent reasons for affirming that it was not.

Regarding the first point Dr. Lightfoot asserts :—

"The first is refuted by a large number of examples. St. Paul, for instance, describes it as the special privilege of the Jews that they had the keeping of 'the oracles of God' (Rom. iii. 2). Can we suppose that he meant anything else but the Old Testament Scriptures by this expression ? Is it possible that he would exclude the books of Genesis, of Joshua, of Samuel and Kings, or only include such fragments of them as professed to give the direct sayings of God ? Would he, or would he not, comprise under the term the account of the creation and fall (1 Cor. xi. 8 *sq.*), of the wanderings in the wilderness (1 Cor. x. 1 *sq.*), of Sarah and Hagar (Gal. iv. 21 *sq.*) ? Does not the main part of his argument in the very next chapter (Rom. iv.) depend more on the narrative of God's dealings than His words ? Again, when the author of the Epistle to the Hebrews refers to 'the first principles of the oracles of God' (v. 12), his meaning is explained by his practice ; for he elicits the Divine teaching quite as much from the history as from the direct precepts of the Old Testament. But if the language of the New Testament writers leaves any loophole for doubt, this is not the case with their contemporary Philo. In one place he speaks of the words in Deut. x. 9, 'The Lord is his inheritance,' as an 'oracle' (λόγιον) ; in another he quotes as an 'oracle' (λόγιον) the *narrative* in Gen. iv. 15 : 'The Lord God set a mark upon Cain, lest anyone finding him should kill him.' [3] From this and other passages it is clear that with Philo an 'oracle' is a synonyme for a Scripture. Similarly Clement of Rome writes : 'Ye know well the sacred Scriptures, and have studied the oracles of God ;' [4] and immediately he recalls to their mind the account in Deut. ix. 12 *sq.*, Exod. xxxii. 7 *sq.*, of which the point is not any Divine precept or prediction, but *the example of Moses.* A

---

[1] *Ibid.* p. 173.   [2] i. 236 ff.   [3] Note.   [4] Note.

few years later Polycarp speaks in condemnation of those who 'pervert the oracles of the Lord.'"[1]

He then goes on to refer to Irenæus, Clement of Alexandria, Origen, and Basil, but I need not follow him to these later writers, but confine myself to that which I have quoted.

"When Paul writes in the Epistle to the Romans iii. 2, 'They were entrusted with the oracles of God,' can he mean anything else but the Old Testament Scriptures, including the historical books?" argues Dr. Lightfoot. I maintain, on the contrary, that he certainly does not refer to a collection of writings at all, but to the communications or revelations of God, and, as the context shows, probably more immediately to the Messianic prophecies. The advantage of the Jews, in fact, according to Paul here, was that to them were first communicated the Divine oracles : that they were made the medium of God's utterances to mankind. There seems almost an echo of the expression in Acts vii. 38, where Stephen is represented as saying to the Jews of their fathers on Mount Sinai, "who received living oracles (λόγια ζῶντα) to give unto us." Of this nature were the "oracles of God" which were entrusted to the Jews. Further, the phrase : "the first principles of the oracles of God" (Heb. v. 12), is no application of the term to narrative, as Dr. Lightfoot affirms, however much the author may illustrate his own teaching by Old Testament history ; but the writer of the Epistle clearly explains his meaning in the first and second verses of his letter, when he says : "God having spoken to the fathers in time past in the prophets, at the end of these days spake unto us in His Son." Dr. Lightfoot also urges that Philo applies the term "oracle" (λόγιον) to the *narrative* in Gen. iv. 15, &c. The fact is, however,

---

[1] Clem. Rom. § 53, § 45; *ibid.* 173 f.

that Philo considered almost every part of the Old Testament as allegorical, and held that narrative or descriptive phrases veiled Divine oracles. When he applies the term " oracle " to any of these it is not to the narrative, but to the Divine utterance which he believes to be mystically contained in it, and which he extracts and expounds in the usual extravagant manner of Alexandrian typologists. Dr. Lightfoot does not refer to the expression of 1 Pet. iv. 11, " Let him speak as the oracles of God " ($\dot{\omega}\varsigma$ $\lambda\acute{o}\gamma\iota\alpha$ $\Theta\epsilon o\hat{v}$), which shows the use of the word in the New Testament. He does point out the passage in the " Epistle of Clement of Rome," than which, in my opinion, nothing could more directly tell against him. " Ye know well the sacred Scriptures and have studied the oracles of God." The " oracles of God " are pointedly distinguished from the sacred Scriptures, of which they form a part. These oracles are contained in the " sacred Scriptures," but are not synonymous with the whole of them. Dr. Light- foot admits that we cannot say how much " Polycarp " included in the expression : " pervert the oracles of the Lord," but I maintain that it must be referred to the teaching of Jesus regarding " a resurrection and a judgment," and not to historical books.

In replying to Dr. Lightfoot's chapter on the Silence of Eusebius, I have said all that is necessary regarding the other Gospels in connection with Papias. Papias is the most interesting witness we have concerning the composition of the Gospels. He has not told us much, but he has told us more than any previous writer. Dr. Lightfoot has not scrupled to discredit his own witness, however, and he is quite right in suggesting that no great reliance can be placed upon his testimony. It comes to this : We cannot rely upon the correctness of the meagre account of the Gospels supposed to have been written by Mark and Matthew, and we have no other upon which to fall back. Regarding the other two Gospels, we have no information whatever from Papias, whether correct or incorrect, and altogether this Father does little or nothing towards establishing the credibility of miracles and the reality of Divine Revelation.

V.

MELITO OF SARDIS—CLAUDIUS APOLLINARIS— POLYCRATES.

THROUGHOUT the whole of these essays, Dr. Lightfoot has shown the most complete misapprehension of the purpose for which the examination of the evidence regarding the Gospels in early writings was undertaken in *Supernatural Religion*, and consequently he naturally misunderstands and misrepresents its argument from first to last. This becomes increasingly evident when we come to writers, whom he fancifully denominates : " the later school of St. John." He evidently considers that he is producing a very destructive effect, when he demonstrates from the writings, genuine or spurious, of such men as Melito of Sardis, Claudius Apollinaris and Polycrates of Ephesus, or from much more than suspected documents like the Martyrdom of Polycarp, that towards the last quarter of the second century they were acquainted with the doctrines of Christianity and, as he infers, derived them from our four Gospels. He really seems incapable of discriminating between a denial that there is clear and palpable evidence of the existence and authorship of these particular Gospels, and denial that they actually existed at all. I do not suppose that there is any critic, past or present, who doubts that our four Gospels had been composed and were in wide circulation during this

K

period of the second century. It is a very different matter to examine what absolute testimony there is regarding the origin, authenticity, and trustworthiness of these documents, as records of miracles and witnesses for the reality of Divine Revelation.

I cannot accuse myself of having misled Dr. Light-foot on this point by any obscurity in the statement of my object, but, as he and other apologists have carefully ignored it, and systematically warped my argument, either by accident or design, I venture to quote a few sentences from *Supernatural Religion*, both to justify myself and to restore the discussion to its proper lines.

In winding up the first part of the work, which was principally concerned with the antecedent credibility of miracles, I said :—

"Now it is apparent that the evidence for miracles requires to embrace two distinct points : the reality of the alleged facts, and the accuracy of the inference that the phenomena were produced by supernatural agency. . . . In order, however, to render our conclusion complete, it remains for us to see whether, as affirmed, there be any special evidence regarding the alleged facts entitling the Gospel miracles to exceptional attention. If, instead of being clear, direct, the undoubted testimony of known eye-witnesses free from superstition and capable, through adequate knowledge, rightly to estimate the alleged phenomena, we find that the actual accounts have none of these qualifications, the final decision with regard to miracles and the reality of Divine Revelation will be easy and conclusive." [1]

Before commencing the examination of the evidence for the Gospels, I was careful to state the principles upon which I considered it right to proceed. I said:—

" Before commencing our examination of the evidence as to the date, authorship, and character of the Gospels, it may be well to make a few preliminary remarks, and clearly state certain canons of

[1] I. p. 210 f.

criticism.   We shall make no attempt to establish any theory as to the date at which any of the Gospels was actually written, but simply examine all the testimony which is extant, with the view of ascertaining *what is known of these works and their authors, certainly and distinctly, as distinguished from what is merely conjectured or inferred*. . . . We propose, therefore, as exhaustively as possible, to search all the writings of the early Church for information regarding the Gospels, and to examine even the alleged indications of their use. . . . It is still more important that we should constantly bear in mind that a great number of Gospels existed in the early Church which are no longer extant, and of most of which even the names are lost.   We need not here do more than refer, in corroboration of this fact, to the preliminary statement of the author of the third Gospel : ' Forasmuch as many (πολλοὶ) took in hand to set forth in order a declaration of the things which have been accomplished among us,' &c.   It is, therefore, evident that before our third synoptic was written many similar works were already in circulation.   Looking at the close similarity of large portions of the three synoptics, it is almost certain that many of the writings here mentioned bore a close analogy to each other and to our Gospels, and this is known to have been the case, for instance, amongst the various forms of the ' Gospel according to the Hebrews.'   When, therefore, in early writings, we meet with quotations closely resembling, or, we may add, even identical, with passages which are found in our Gospels, the source of which, however, is not mentioned, nor is any author's name indicated, *the similarity or even identity cannot by any means be admitted as proof that the quotation is necessarily from our Gospels, and not from some other similar work now no longer extant,* and more especially not when, in the same writings, there are other quotations from sources different from our Gospels. . . . But whilst similarity to our Gospels in passages quoted by early writers from unnamed sources cannot *prove* the use of our Gospels, variation from them would suggest or prove a different origin, *and at least it is obvious that anonymous quotations which do not agree with our Gospels cannot in any case necessarily indicate their existence*. . . . It is unnecessary to add that, in proportion as we remove from Apostolic times without positive evidence of the existence and authenticity of our Gospels, so does the value of their testimony dwindle away.   Indeed, requiring, as we do, clear, direct and irrefragable evidence of the integrity, authenticity, and historical character of these Gospels, doubt or obscurity on these points must inevitably be fatal to them as sufficient testimony—if they could, under any circumstances, be considered sufficient testimony

—for miracles and a direct Divine Revelation like ecclesiastical Christianity." [1]

Dr. Lightfoot must have been aware of these statements, since he has made the paragraph on the silence of ancient writers the basis of his essay on the silence of Eusebius, and has been so particular in calling attention to any alteration I have made in my text; and it might have been better if, instead of cheap sneers on every occasion in which these canons have been applied, he had once for all stated any reasons which he can bring forward against the canons themselves. The course he has adopted, I can well understand, is more convenient for him and, after all, with many it is quite as effective.

It may be well that I should here again illustrate the necessity for such canons of criticism as I have indicated above, and which can be done very simply from our own Gospels :—

"Not only the language but the order of a quotation must have its due weight, and we have no right to dismember a passage and, discovering fragmentary parallels in various parts of the Gospels, to assert that it is compiled from them and not derived, as it stands, from another source. As an illustration, let us for a moment suppose the 'Gospel according to Luke' to have been lost, like the 'Gospel according to the Hebrews' and so many others. In the works of one of the Fathers we discover the following quotation from an unnamed evangelical work : 'And he said unto them (ἔλεγεν δὲ πρὸς αὐτούς) : The harvest truly is great, but the labourers are few ; pray ye therefore the Lord of the harvest that he would send forth labourers into his harvest. Go your ways (ὑπάγετε) : behold, I send you forth as lambs (ἄρνας) in the midst of wolves.' Following the system adopted in regard to Justin and others, apologetic critics would of course maintain that this was a compilation from memory of passages quoted from our first Gospel—that is to say, Matt ix. 37 : 'Then saith he unto his disciples (τότε λέγει τοῖς μαθηταῖς αὐτοῦ), The harvest,' &c.; and Matt. x. 16 : 'Behold, I (ἐγὼ) send you forth as sheep (πρόβατα) in the midst of wolves : be ye

---

[1] I. p. 213 ff. I have italicised a few phrases.

therefore,' &c., which, with the differences which we have indicated, agree. It would probably be in vain to argue that the quotation indicated a continuous order, and the variations combined to confirm the probability of a different source, and still more so to point out that, although parts of the quotation, separated from their context, might, to a certaint extent, correspond with scattered verses in the first Gospel, such a circumstance was no proof that the quotation was taken from that and from no other Gospel. The passage, however, is a literal quotation from Luke x. 2–3, which, as we have assumed, had been lost.

"Again, still supposing the third Gospel no longer extant, we might find the following quotation in a work of the Fathers : 'Take heed to yourselves (ἑαυτοῖς) of the leaven of the Pharisees, which is hypocrisy (ἥτις ἐστὶν ὑπόκρισις). For there is nothing covered up (συγκεκαλυμμένον) which shall not be revealed, and hid, which shall not be known.' It would, of course, be affirmed that this was evidently a combination of two verses of our first Gospel quoted almost literally, with merely a few very immaterial slips of memory in the parts we note, and the explanatory words, 'which is hypocrisy,' introduced by the Father, and not a part of the quotation at all. The two verses are Matt. xvi. 6, 'Beware and take heed (ὁρᾶτε καὶ) of the leaven of the Pharisees and Sadducees (καὶ Σαδδουκαίων), and Matt. x. 26, '. . . for (γὰρ) there is nothing covered (κεκαλυμμένον) that shall not be revealed, and hid, that shall not be known.' The sentence would, in fact, be divided as in the case of Justin, and each part would have its parallel pointed out in separate portions of the Gospel. How wrong such a system is—and it is precisely that which is adopted with regard to Justin—is clearly established by the fact that the quotation, instead of being such a combination, is simply taken as it stands from the 'Gospel according to Luke,' xii. 1–2." [1]

"If we examine further, however, in the same way, quotations which differ merely in language, we arrive at the very same conclusion. Supposing the third Gospel to be lost, what would be the source assigned to the following quotation from an unnamed Gospel in the work of one of the Fathers ? 'No servant (οὐδεὶς οἰκέτης) can serve two lords, for either he will hate the one and love the other, or else he will hold to the one and despise the other. Ye cannot serve God and Mammon.' Of course the passage would be claimed as a quotation from memory of Matt. vi. 24, with which it perfectly corresponds, with the exception of the addition of the second word,

[1] *S. R.* i. 259 ff. See further illustrations here.

οἰκέτης, which, it would no doubt be argued, is an evident and very natural amplification of the simple οὐδείς of the first Gospel. Yet this passage, only differing by the single word from Matthew, is a literal quotation from the Gospel according to Luke xvi. 13. Or, to take another instance, supposing the third Gospel to be lost, and the following passage quoted, from an unnamed source, by one of the Fathers : 'Beware (προσέχετε) of the Scribes, which desire to walk in long robes, and love (φιλούντων) greetings in the markets, and chief seats in the synagogues, and chief places at feasts ; which devour widows' houses, and for a pretence make long prayers : these shall receive greater damnation.' This would, without hesitation, be declared a quotation from memory of Mark xii. 38–40, from which it only differs in a couple of words. It is, however, a literal quotation of Luke xx. 46–47, yet probably it would be in vain to submit to apologetic critics that possibly, not to say probably, the passage was not derived from Mark, but from a lost Gospel. To quote one more instance, let us suppose the 'Gospel according to Mark' no longer extant, and that in some early work there existed the following passage : 'It is easier for a camel to go through the eye (τρυμαλιᾶς) of a needle than for a rich man to enter into the kingdom of God.' This of course would be claimed as a quotation from memory of Matt. xix. 24, with which it agrees with the exception of the substitution of τρυπήματος for τρυμαλιᾶς. It would not the less have been an exact quotation from Mark x. 25." [1]

Illustrations of this kind could be indefinitely multiplied, and to anyone who has studied the three synoptics, with their similarities and variations, and considered the probable mode of their compilation, it must be apparent that, with the knowledge that very many other Gospels existed (Luke i. 1), which can only very slowly have disappeared from circulation, it is impossible for anyone with a due appreciation of the laws of evidence to assert that the use of short passages similar to others in our Gospels actually proves that they must have been derived from these alone, and cannot have emanated from any other source. It is not necessary to deny that they may equally have come

[1] *S. R.* i. p. 303 f.

from the Gospels, but the inevitable decision of a judicial mind, seriously measuring evidence, must be that they do not absolutely prove anything.

Coming now more directly to the essay on "The later school of St. John," it is curious to find Dr. Lightfoot setting in the very foreground the account of Polycarp's martyrdom, without a single word regarding the more than suspicious character of the document, except the remark in a note that "the objections which have been urged against this narrative are not serious."[1] They have been considered so by men like Keim, Schürer, Lipsius, and Holtzmann. The account has too much need to be propped up itself to be of much use as a prop for the Gospels. Dr. Lightfoot points out that an "idea of literal conformity to the life and Passion of Christ runs through the document,"[2] and it is chiefly on the fact that "most of the incidents have their counterparts in the circumstances of the Passion, as recorded by the synoptic evangelists alone or in common with St. John," that he relies, in referring to the martyrdom. I need scarcely reply that not only, on account of the very doubtful character of the document, is it useless to us as evidence, but because it does not name a single Gospel, much less add anything to our knowledge of their authorship and trustworthiness. I shall have more to say regarding Dr. Lightfoot in connection with this document further on.

The same remark applies to Melito of Sardis. I have fully discussed[3] the evidence which he is supposed to contribute, and it is unnecessary for me to enter into it at any length here, more especially as Dr. Lightfoot does not advance any new argument. He has said nothing which materially alters the doubtful position

---

[1] *S. R.* ii. p. 221, n. 7.   [2] *Ibid.* p. 220.   [3] *Ibid.* ii. p. 169 f.

of many of the fragments attributed to this Father.   In
any case the use which Dr. Lightfoot chiefly makes of
him as a witness is to show that Melito exhibits full
knowledge of the details of evangelical history as contained in the four canonical Gospels.   Waiving all
discussion of the authenticity of the fragments, and
accepting, for the sake of argument, the asserted acquaintance with evangelical history which they display,
I simply enquire what this proves?   Does anyone
doubt that Melito of Sardis, in the last third of the
second century, must have been thoroughly versed in
Gospel history, or deny that he might have possessed
our four Gospels?   The only thing which is lacking is
actual proof of the fact. ' Melito does not refer to a
single Gospel by name.   He does not add one word or
one fact to our knowledge of the Gospels or their composers.   He does not, indeed, mention any writing of the
New Testament.   If his words regarding the " Books of
the Old Testament " imply " a corresponding Christian
literature which he regarded as the books of the New
Testament," [1] which I deny, what is gained?   Even in
that case " we cannot," as Dr. Lardner frankly states,
" infer the names or the exact number of those books."
As for adding anything to the credibility of miracles,
such an idea is not even broached by Dr. Lightfoot, and
yet if he cannot do this the only purpose for which his
testimony is examined is gone.   The elaborate display
of vehemence in discussing the authenticity of fragments
of his writings merely distracts the attention of the
reader from the true issue if, when established to his
own satisfaction, Dr. Lightfoot cannot turn the evidence
of Melito to greater account.[2]

---

[1] *S. R.* ii. p. 226.
[2] In discussing the authenticity of fragments ascribed to Melito, Dr.
Lightfoot quoted, as an argument from *Supernatural Religion*, the following

Nor is he much more fortunate in the case of Claudius Apollinaris,[1] whose " Apology " may be dated about A.D. 177–180. In an extract preserved in the *Paschal Chronicle*, regarding the genuineness of which all discussion may, for the sake of argument, be waived here, the writer in connection with the Paschal Festival says that " they affirm that Matthew represents " one thing " and, on their showing, the Gospels seem to be at variance with one another." [2] If, therefore, the passage be genuine, the writer seems to refer to the first synoptic, and by inference to the fourth Gospel. He says nothing of the composition of these works, and he does nothing more than merely show that they were accepted in his time. This may seem a good deal when we consider how very few of his contemporaries do as much, but it really contributes nothing to our knowledge of the authors, and does not add a jot to their credibility as witnesses for miracles and the reality of Divine Revelation.

With regard to Polycrates of Ephesus I need say very little. Eusebius preserves a passage from a letter which he wrote " in the closing years of the second century," [3] when Victor of Rome attempted to force the Western usage with respect to Easter on the Asiatic Christians. In this he uses the expression " he that leaned on the bosom of the Lord," which occurs in the fourth Gospel. Nothing could more forcibly show the meagreness of our information regarding the Gospels

words: " They have, in fact, no attestation whatever except that of the Syriac translation, which is unknown and which, therefore, is worthless." The passage appeared thus in the *Contemporary Review*, and now is again given in the same form in the present volume. I presume that the passage which Dr. Lightfoot intends to quote is: " They have no attestation whatever, except that of the Syriac translator, who is unknown, and which is, therefore, worthless " (*S. R.* ii. p. 181). If Dr. Lightfoot, who has so much assistance in preparing his works for the press, can commit such mistakes, he ought to be a little more charitable to those who have none.

[1] *S. R.* ii. p. 182 ff.   [2] *Ibid.* p. 230.   [3] *Ibid.* p. 248.

than that such a phrase is considered of value as evidence for one of them.   In fact, the slightness of our knowledge of these works is perfectly astounding when the importance which is attached to them is taken into account.

VI.

THE CHURCHES OF GAUL.

A SEVERE persecution broke out in the year A.D. 177, under Marcus Aurelius, in the cities of Vienne and Lyons, on the Rhone, and an account of the martyrdoms which then took place was given in a letter from the persecuted communities, addressed "to the brethren that are in Asia and Phrygia." This epistle is in great part preserved to us by Eusebius (*H. E.* v. 1), and it is to a consideration of its contents that Dr. Lightfoot devotes his essay on the Churches of Gaul. But for the sake of ascertaining clearly what evidence actually exists of the Gospels, it would have been of little utility to extend the enquiry in *Supernatural Religion* to this document, written nearly a century and a half after the death of Jesus, but it is instructive to show how exceedingly slight is the information we possess regarding those documents. I may at once say that no writing of the New Testament is directly referred to by name in this epistle, and consequently any supposed quotations are merely inferred to be such by their similarity to passages found in these writings. With the complete unconsciousness which I have pointed out that Dr. Lightfoot affects regarding the object and requirements of my argument, Dr. Lightfoot is, of course, indignant that I will not accept as conclusive evidence the imper-

fect coincidences which alone he is able to bring forward. I have elsewhere fully discussed these,[1] and I
need only refer to some portions of his essay here.

"Of Vettius Epagathus, one of the sufferers, we are told that,
though young, he 'rivalled the testimony borne to the elder Zacharias (συνεξισοῦσθαι τῇ τοῦ πρεσβυτέρου Ζαχαρίου μαρτυρίᾳ), for verily
(γοῦν) he had *walked in all the commandments and ordinances of
the Lord blameless.*' Here we have the same words, and in the same
order, which are used of Zacharias and Elizabeth in St. Luke (i. 6) :
'and Zacharias, his father, was filled with the Holy Ghost.'"[2]

Dr. Lightfoot very properly dwells on the meaning
of the expression " the testimony of Zacharias " (τῇ
τοῦ Ζαχαρίου μαρτυρίᾳ), which he points out " might
signify either 'the testimony borne to Zacharias,' *i.e.*
his recorded character, or 'the testimony borne by
Zacharias,' *i.e.* his martyrdom." By a vexatious mistake in reprinting, " to " was accidentally substituted
for " by " in my translation of this passage in a very
few of the earlier copies of my sixth edition, but the
error was almost immediately observed and corrected
in the rest of the edition. Dr. Lightfoot seizes upon
the " to " in the early copy which I had sent to him,
and argues upon it as a deliberate adoption of the interpretation, whilst he takes me to task for actually
arguing upon the rendering "by" in my text. Very
naturally a printer's error could not extend to my argument. The following is what I say regarding the
passage in my complete edition :—

"The epistle is an account of the persecution of the Christian
community of Vienne and Lyons, and Vettius Epagathus is the
first of the martyrs who is named in it : μαρτυρία was at that time
the term used to express the supreme testimony of Christians—
martyrdom—and the epistle seems here simply to refer to the martyrdom, the honour of which he shared with Zacharias. It is, we
think, highly improbable that, under such circumstances, the word

---

[1] *S. R.* ii. p. 108 ff., iii. 24 ff.   [2] *Ibid.* 255.

μαρτυρία would have been used to express a mere description of the character of Zacharias given by some other writer."

This is the interpretation which is adopted by Tischendorf, Hilgenfeld, and many eminent critics.

It will be observed that the saying that he had "walked in all the commandments and ordinances of the Lord blameless," which is supposed to be taken from Luke i. 6, is there applied to Zacharias and Elizabeth, the father and mother of John the Baptist, but the Gospel does not say anything of this Zacharias having suffered martyrdom. The allusion in Luke xi. 51 (Matt. xxiii. 35) is almost universally admitted to be to another Zacharias, whose martyrdom is related in 2 Chron. xxiv. 21.

"Since the epistle, therefore, refers to the martyrdom of Zacharias, the father of John the Baptist, when using the expressions which are supposed to be taken from our third synoptic, is it not reasonable to suppose that those expressions were derived from some work which likewise contained an account of his death, which is not found in the synoptic? When we examine the matter more closely we find that, although none of the canonical gospels except the third gives any narrative of the birth of John the Baptist, that portion of the Gospel in which are the words we are discussing cannot be considered an original production by the third Synoptist, but, like the rest of his work, is merely a composition based upon earlier written narratives. Ewald, for instance, assigns the whole of the first chapters of Luke (i. 5–ii. 40) to what he terms 'the eighth recognisable book.'"[1]

No apologetic critic pretends that the author of the third Gospel can have written this account from his own knowledge or observation. Where, then, did he get his information? Surely not from oral tradition limited to himself. The whole character of the narrative, even apart from the prologue to the Gospel, and the composition of the rest of the work, would lead us to infer a written source.

[1] *S. R.* ii. p. 200.

"The fact that other works existed at an earlier period in which the history of Zacharias, the father of the Baptist, was given, and in which not only the words used in the epistle were found, but also the martyrdom, is in the highest degree probable, and, so far as the history is concerned, this is placed almost beyond doubt by the 'Protevangelium Jacobi,' which contains it. Tischendorf, who does not make use of this epistle at all as evidence for the Scriptures of the New Testament, does refer to it, and to this very allusion in it to the martyrdom of Zacharias, as testimony to the existence and use of the 'Protevangelium Jacobi,' a work whose origin he dates so far back as the first three decades of the second century, and which he considers was also used by Justin, as Hilgenfeld had already observed. Tischendorf and Hilgenfeld, therefore, agree in affirming that the reference to Zacharias which we have quoted indicates acquaintance with a Gospel different from our third synoptic." [1]

Such being the state of the case, I would ask any impartial reader whether there is any evidence here that these few words, introduced without the slightest indication of the source from which they were derived, must have been quoted from our third Gospel, and cannot have been taken from some one of the numerous evangelical works in circulation before that Gospel was written. The reply of everyone accustomed to weigh evidence must be that the words cannot even prove the existence of our synoptic at the time the letter was written.

"But, if our author disposes of the coincidences with the third Gospel in this way" (proceeds Dr. Lightfoot), "what will he say to those with the Acts? In this same letter of the Gallican Churches we are told that the sufferers prayed for their persecutors 'like Stephen, the perfect martyr, "Lord, lay not this sin to their charge."' Will he boldly maintain that the writers had before them another Acts, containing words identical with our Acts, just as he supposes them to have had another Gospel, containing words identical with our Third Gospel? Or, will he allow this account to have been taken from Acts vii. 60, with which it coincides? But in this latter case, if they had the second treatise, which bears the name of St.

[1] *S. R.* ii. p. 200 f.

Luke, in their hands, why should they not have had the first also ? " [1]

My reply to this is :—

" There is no mention of the Acts of the Apostles in the epistle, and the source from which the writers obtained their information about Stephen, is, of course, not stated. If there really was a martyr of the name of Stephen, and if these words were actually spoken by him, the tradition of the fact, and the memory of his noble saying, may well have remained in the Church, or have been recorded in writings then current, from one of which, indeed, eminent critics (as Bleek, Ewald, Meyer, Neander, De Wette) conjecture that the author of Acts derived his materials, and in this case the passage obviously does not prove the use of the Acts. If, on the other hand, there never was such a martyr by whom the words were spoken, and the whole story must be considered an original invention by the author of Acts, then, in that case, and in that case only, the passage does show the use of the Acts. Supposing that the use of Acts be held to be thus indicated, what does this prove ? Merely that the ' Acts of the Apostles ' were in existence in the year 177–178, when the epistle of Vienne and Lyons was written. No light whatever would thus be thrown upon the question of its authorship ; and neither its credibility nor its sufficiency to prove the reality of a cycle of miracles would be in the slightest degree established." [2]

Apart from the question of the sufficiency of evidence actually under examination, however, I have never suggested, much less asserted, that the " Acts of the Apostles " was not in existence at this date. The only interest attachable to the question is, as I have before said, the paucity of the testimony regarding the book, to demonstrate which it has been necessary to discuss all such supposed allusions. But the apologetic argument characteristically ignores the fact that " many took in hand " at an early date to set forth the Christian story, and that the books of our New Testament did not constitute the whole of Christian literature in circulation in the early days of the Church.

[1] *S. R.* iii. p. 257. [2] *Ibid.* iii. p. 25 f.

I need not go with any minuteness into the alleged quotation from the fourth Gospel. " There shall come a time in which whosoever killeth you will think that he doeth God service." The Gospel has: " There cometh an hour when," &c., and, as no source is named, it is useless to maintain that the use of this Gospel, and the impossibility of the use of any other, is proved. If even this were conceded, the passage does not add one iota to our knowledge of the authorship and credibility of the Gospel. Dr. Lightfoot says : " The author of *Supernatural Religion* maintains, on the other hand, that only twelve years before, at the outside, the very Church to which Irenæus belonged, in a public document with which he was acquainted, betrays no knowledge of our canonical Gospels, but quotes from one or more apocryphal Gospels instead. He maintains this though the quotations in question are actually found in our canonical Gospels." [1] Really, Dr. Lightfoot betrays that he has not understood the argument, which merely turns upon the insufficiency of the evidence to prove the use of particular documents, whilst others existed which possibly, or probably, did contain similar passages to those in debate.

[1] *Ibid.,* p. 259.

VII.

TATIAN'S 'DIATESSARON.'

I NEED not reply at any length to Dr. Lightfoot's essay on the *Diatessaron* of Tatian, and I must refer those who wish to see what I had to say on the subject to *Supernatural Religion*.[1] I may here confine myself to remarks connected with fresh matter which has appeared since the publication of my work.

An Armenian translation of what is alleged to be the Commentary of Ephraem Syrus on Tatian's *Diatessaron* was published as long ago as 1836, but failed to attract critical attention. In 1876, however, a Latin translation of this work by Aucher and Moesinger was issued, and this has now naturally introduced new elements into the argument regarding Tatian's use of Gospels. Only last year, a still more important addition to critical materials was made by the publication in Rome of an alleged Arabic version of Tatian's *Diatessaron* itself, with a Latin translation by Ciasca. These works were not before Dr. Lightfoot when he wrote his Essay on Tatian in 1877, and he only refers to them in a note in his present volume. He entertains no doubt as to the genuineness of these works, and he triumphantly .claims that they establish the truth of

---

[1] II. pp. 144 ff., 372 ff.

L

the " ecclesiastical theory " regarding the *Diatessaron*
of Tatian.

In order to understand the exact position of the case,
however, it will be well to state again what is known
regarding Tatian's work.   Eusebius is the first writer
who mentions it.   He says—and to avoid all dispute
I give Dr. Lightfoot's rendering :—

> " Tatian composed a sort of connection and compilation, I know
> not how (οὐκ οἶδ' ὅπως), of the Gospels, and called it *Diatessaron*.
> This work is current in some quarters (with some persons) even to
> the present day." [1]

I argued that this statement indicates that Eusebius
was not personally acquainted with the work in question,
but speaks of it from mere hearsay.   Dr. Lightfoot
replies—

> " His inference, however, from the expression ' I know not how '
> is altogether unwarranted.   So far from implying that Eusebius had
> no personal knowledge of the work, it is constantly used by writers
> in speaking of books where they are perfectly acquainted with the
> contents, but do not understand the principles, or do not approve
> the method.   In idiomatic English it signifies ' I cannot think what
> he was about,' and is equivalent to ' unaccountably,' ' absurdly,' so
> that, if anything, it implies knowledge rather than ignorance of the
> contents.   I have noticed at least twenty-six examples of its use in
> the treatise of Origen against Celsus alone,[2] where it commonly
> refers to Celsus' work which he had before him, and very often to
> passages which he himself quotes in the context." [3]

If this signification be also attached to the expression,
it is equally certain that οὐκ οἶδ' ὅπως is used to express ignorance, although Dr. Lightfoot chooses, for the
sake of his argument, to forget the fact.   In any case
some of the best critics draw the same inference from the
phrase here that I do, more especially as Eusebius does
not speak further or more definitely of the *Diatessaron*,

---

[1] Euseb. *H. E.* iv. 29.   (*Ibid.* p. 227 f.)
[2] I need not quote the references which Dr. Lightfoot gives in a note.
[3] *Ibid.* p. 278.

amongst whom I may name Credner, Hilgenfeld, Holz-
mann, Reuss and Scholten ; and should these not have
weight with him I may refer Dr. Lightfoot to Zahn,[1]
and even to Dr. Westcott [2] and Professor Hemphill.[3]
Eusebius says nothing more of the *Diatessaron* of
Tatian and gives us no further help towards a recognition of the work.

Dr. Lightfoot supposes that I had overlooked the
testimony of the *Doctrine of Addai*, an apocryphal
Syriac work, published in 1876 by Dr. Phillips after
Supernatural Religion was written.   I did not overlook
it, but I considered it of too little critical value to require much notice in later editions of the work.   The
Doctrine of Addai is conjecturally dated by Dr. Lightfoot about the middle of the third century,[4] and it might
with greater certainty be placed much later.   The
passage to which he points is one in which it is said
that the new converts meet together to hear, along with
the Old Testament, " the New of the *Diatessaron*."   This
is assumed to be Tatian's " Harmony of the Gospels,"
and I shall not further argue the point ; but does it
bring us any nearer to a certain understanding of its
character and contents ?

The next witness, taking them in the order in
which Dr. Lightfoot cites them, is Dionysius Bar-Salibi,
who flourished in the last years of the twelfth century.
In his commentary on the Gospels he writes :—

" Tatian, the disciple of Justin, the philosopher and martyr,
selected and patched together from the four Gospels and constructed
a gospel, which he called *Diatessaron*—that is, *Miscellanies*.   On this
work Mar Ephraem wrote an exposition ; and its commencement
was—*In the beginning was the Word*.   Elias of Salamia, who is
also called Aphthonius, constructed a gospel after the likeness of the

---

[1] *Unters. N. T. Kanons*, 1881, p. 15 f.
[2] *On the Canon*, 1875, p. 318, n. 3.   Cf. 1881, p. 322, n. 3.
[3] *The Diatessaron of Tatian*, 1888, p. xiv.   [4] *Ibid.* p. 279.

Diatessaron of Ammonius, mentioned by Eusebius in his prologue to the Canons which he made for the Gospel. Elias sought for that *Diatessaron* and could not find it, and in consequence constructed this after its likeness. And the said Elias finds fault with several things in the Canons of Eusebius, and points out errors in them, and rightly. But this copy (work) which Elias composed is not often met with." [1]

This information regarding Ephraem—who died about A.D. 373—be it remembered, is given by a writer of the twelfth century, and but for this we should not have known from any ancient independent source that Ephraem had composed a commentary at all, supposing that he did so. It is important to note, however, that a second *Diatessaron*, prepared by Ammonius, is here mentioned, and that it was also described by Eusebius in his Epistle to Carpianus, and further that Bar-Salibi speaks of a third, composed on the same lines by Elias. Dr. Lightfoot disposes of the *Diatessaron* of Ammonius in a very decided way. He says :—

"It was quite different in its character from the *Diatessaron* of Tatian. The *Diatessaron* of Tatian was a patchwork of the four Gospels, commencing with the preface of St. John. The work of Ammonius took the Gospel of St. Matthew as its standard, preserving its continuity, and placed side by side with it parallel passages from the other Gospels. The principle of the one was *amalgamation* ; of the other, *comparison*. No one who had seen the two works could confuse them, though they bore the same name, *Diatessaron*. Eusebius keeps them quite distinct. So does Bar-Salibi. Later on in his commentary, we are told, he quotes both works in the same place." [2]

Doubtless, no one comparing the two works here described could confuse them, but it is far from being so clear that anyone who had not seen more than one of these works could with equal certainty distinguish it. The statement of Dr. Lightfoot quoted above, that

---

[1] Dr. Lightfoot's rendering, p. 280.   Asscm. *Bibl. Orient.* ii. p. 159 sq.
[2] *Ibid.* p. 280 f.

the *Diatessaron* of Ammonius "took the Gospel of St. Matthew as its standard, preserving its continuity," certainly does not tend to show that it was "quite different in its character from the *Diatessaron* of Tatian," on the supposition that the Arabic translation lately published represents the work of Tatian. I will quote what Professor Hemphill says regarding it, in preference to making any statement of my own :—

> "On examining the *Diatessaron* as translated into Latin from this Arabic, we find in by far the greater portion of it, from the Sermon on the Mount to the Last Supper (§§ 30–134) that Tatian, like his brother harmonist Ammonius, took St. Matthew as the basis of his work. . . . St. Mark, as might be expected, runs parallel with St. Matthew in the *Diatessaron*, and is in a few cases the source out of which incidents have been incorporated. St. Luke, on the other hand, is employed by Tatian, as also in a lesser degree is St. John, in complete defiance of chronological order." [1]

This is not quite so different from the description of the *Diatessaron* of Ammonius, which Dr. Lightfoot quotes :—

> "He placed side by side with the Gospel according to Matthew the corresponding passages of the other Evangelists, so that as a necessary result the connection of sequence in the three was destroyed so far as regards the order (texture) of reading." [2]

The next witness cited is Theodoret, Bishop of Cyrus, writing about A.D. 453, and I need not quote the well-known passage in which he describes the suppression of some 200 copies of Tatian's work in his diocese, which were in use "not only among persons belonging to his sect, but also among those who follow the Apostolic doctrine," who did not perceive the heretical purpose of a book in which the genealogies and other passages showing the Lord to have been born of

---

[1] *The Diatessaron of Tatian*, p. xxx.
[2] Euseb. *Op.* iv. p. 1276 (ed. Migne.) The translation is by Dr. Lightfoot (*l.c.* p. 281, n. 1).

the seed of David after the flesh were suppressed.   It
is a fact, however, which even Zahn points out, that, in
the alleged *Diatessaron* of Ephraem, these passages are
not all excised, but still remain part of the text,[1] as
they also do in the Arabic translation.   This is the only
definite information which we possess of the contents of
the *Diatessaron* beyond the opening words, and it does
not tally with the recently discovered works.

I need not further discuss here the statement of
Epiphanius that some called Tatian's *Diatessaron* the
Gospel according to the Hebrews.   Epiphanius had not
seen the work himself, and he leaves us in the same
ignorance as to its character.

It is clear from all this that we have no detailed
information regarding the *Diatessaron* of Tatian.   As
Dr. Donaldson said long ago : " We should not be able to
identify it, even if it did come down to us, unless it told
us something reliable about itself." [2]

We may now come to the documents recently published.   The MS. of the Armenian version of the commentary ascribed to Ephraem is dated A.D. 1195, and
Moesinger declares that it is translated from the Syriac,
of which it is said to retain many traces.[3]   He states that
in the judgment of the Mechitarist Fathers the translation dates from about the fifth century,[4] but an opinion
on such a point can only be received with great caution.
The name of Tatian is not mentioned as the author of
the " Harmony," and the question is open as to whether
the authorship of the commentary is rightly ascribed to
Ephraem Syrus.   In any case there can be no doubt that
the Armenian work is a translation.

The Arabic work published by Ciasca, and sup-

---

[1] Zahn, *Tatian's Diatessaron*, 1881, p. 70 f.
[2] *Hist. Chr. Lit. and Doctr.* iii. p. 26.
[3] Moesinger, *Evang. Concor. Expositio*, 1876, p. x f.   [4] *Ibid.* p. xi.

posed to be a version of Tatian's *Diatessaron* itself, is
derived from two manuscripts, one belonging to the
Vatican Library and the other forwarded to Rome
from Egypt by the Vicar Apostolic of the Catholic Copts.
The latter MS. states, in notes at the beginning and end,
that it is an Arabic translation of the *Diatessaron* of
Tatian, made from the Syriac by the presbyter Abû-l-
Pharag Abdullah Ben-at-Tib, who is believed to have
flourished in the first half of the eleventh century, and
in one of these notes the name of the scribe who wrote
the Syriac copy is given, which leads to the conjecture
that it may have been dated about the end of the ninth
century. A note in the Vatican MS. also ascribes the
original work to Tatian. These notes constitute the
principal or only ground for connecting Tatian's name
with the "Harmony."

So little is known regarding the *Diatessaron* of
Tatian that even the language in which it was written
is matter of vehement debate. The name would, of
course, lead to the conclusion that it was a Greek composition, and many other circumstances support this,
but the mere fact that it does not seem to have been
known to Greek Fathers, and that it is very doubtful
whether any of them, with the exception of Theodoret,
had ever seen it, has led many critics to maintain that
it was written in Syriac. Nothing but circumstantial
evidence of this can be produced. This alone shows
how little we really know of the original. The recently
discovered works, being in Arabic and Armenian, even
supposing them to be translations from the Syriac and
that the *Diatessaron* was composed in Syriac, can only
indirectly represent the original, and they obviously
labour under fatal disability in regard to a restoration
of the text of the documents at the basis of the work.
Between doubtful accuracy of rendering and evident

work of revision, the original matter cannot but be
seriously disfigured.

It is certain that the name of Tatian did not appear
as the author of the *Diatessaron*.[1] This is obvious from
the very nature of the composition and its object. We
have met with three works of this description and it is
impossible to say how many more may not have existed.
As the most celebrated, by name at least, it is almost
certain that, as time went on and the identity of such
works was lost, the first idea of anyone meeting with
such a Harmony must have been that it was the *Diatessaron* of Tatian. What means could there be of
correcting it and positively ascertaining the truth? It
is not as if such a work were a personal composition,
showing individuality of style and invention; but supposing it to be a harmony of Gospels already current,
and consequently varying from similar harmonies merely
in details of compilation and arrangement, how is it
possible its authorship could remain in the least degree
certain, in the absence of an arranger's name?

An illustration of all this is aptly supplied in the
case of Victor of Capua, and I will allow Dr. Lightfoot
himself to tell the story.

" Victor, who flourished about A.D. 545, happened to stumble
upon an anonymous Harmony or Digest of the Gospels, and began
in consequence to investigate the authorship. He found two notices
in Eusebius of such Harmonies; one in the *Epistle to Carpianus*
prefixed to the canons, relating to the work of Ammonius; another
in the *Ecclesiastical History*, relating to that of Tatian. Assuming
that the work which he had discovered must be one or other, he
decides in favour of the latter, because it does not give St. Matthew
continuously and append the passages of the other evangelists, as
Eusebius states Ammonius to have done. All this Victor tells us
in the preface to this anonymous Harmony, which he publishes in a
Latin dress.

" There can be no doubt that Victor was mistaken about the

1 Zahn, *l.c.* p. 38.

authorship ; for though the work is constructed on the same general plan as Tatian's, it does not begin with John i. 1, but with Luke i. 1, and it does contain the genealogies.   It belongs, therefore, at least in its present form, neither to Tatian nor to Ammonius." [1]

How this reasoning would have fallen to the ground had the Harmonist, as he might well have done in imitation of Tatian, commenced with the words, " In the beginning was the Word " !   The most instructive part is still to come, however, for although in May 1887 Dr. Lightfoot says : " There can be no doubt that Victor was mistaken about the authorship," &c., in a note now inserted at the end of the essay, after referring to the newly-discovered works, he adds: "On the relation of Victor's *Diatessaron, which seems to be shown after all not to be independent of Tatian*. . . . See Hemphill's *Diatessaron*." [2] On turning to Professor Hemphill's work, the following passage on the point is discovered :—

" It will be remembered that Victor, Bishop of Capua, in the year 543, found a Latin Harmony or compilation of the four Gospels without any name or title, and being a man of enquiring mind he at once set about the task of discovering its unknown author. I have already mentioned the way in which, from the passage of Eusebius, he was led to ascribe his discovery to Tatian. This conclusion was generally traversed by Church writers, and Victor was supposed to have made a mistake. He is now, however, proved to have been a better judge than his critics, for, as Dr. Wace was the first to point out, a comparison of this Latin Harmony with the Ephraem fragments demonstrates their substantial identity, as they preserve to a wonderful degree the same order, and generally proceed *pari passu*." [3]

But how about Luke i. 1 as the beginning ? and the genealogies ? Nothing could more clearly show the uncertainty which must always prevail about such works. Shall we one day discover that Victor was equally right about the reading *Diapente* ?

---

[1] *Ibid.* p. 286.   [2] *Ibid.* p. 288.   The italics are mine.
[3] Hemphill, *The Diatessaron of Tatian*, p. xxiv.

I have thought it worth while to go into all this with a view of showing how little we know of the *Diatessaron* of Tatian and, I may add, of the Commentary of Ephraem Syrus and the work on which it is based. It is not at present necessary to examine more closely the text of either of the recently published works, but, whilst leaving them to be tried by time, I may clearly state what the effect on my argument would be on the assumption made by Dr. Lightfoot that we have actually recovered the *Diatessaron* of Tatian, and that it is composed upon a text more or less corresponding with our four Gospels. Neither in the " Harmony " itself nor in the supposed Commentary of Ephraem Syrus is the name of any of the Evangelists mentioned, and much less is there any information given as to their personality, character, or trustworthiness. If these works were, therefore, the veritable *Diatessaron* of Tatian and the Commentary of Ephraem upon it, the Gospels would not be rendered more credible as the record of miracles nor as witnesses for the reality of Divine Revelation.

It may not be uninstructive if I take the liberty of quoting here some arguments of Dr. Lightfoot regarding the authenticity of the "Letter of the Smyrnaens," giving an account of the martyrdom of Polycarp.[1]

"The miraculous element has also been urged in some quarters as an objection to the genuineness of the document. Yet, considering all the circumstances of the case, we have more occasion to be surprised at the comparative absence than at the special prominence of the supernatural in the narrative. Compared with records of early Christian martyrs, or with biographies of mediæval saints, or with notices of religious heroes at any great crisis, even in the more recent history of the Church—as, for instance, the rise of Jesuitism

---

[1] I have already referred to this document further back, p. 136.

or of Wesleyanism—this document contains nothing which ought to excite a suspicion as to its authenticity.

"The one miraculous incident, which creates a real difficulty, is the dove issuing from the wounded side of the martyr. Yet even this might be accounted for by an illusion, and under any circumstances it would be quite inadequate to condemn the document as a forgery. But it will be shown hereafter (p. 627) that there are excellent reasons for regarding the incident as a later interpolation, which had no place in the original document. Beyond this we have the voice from heaven calling to Polycarp in the stadium to play the man (§ 9). But the very simplicity of the narrative here disarms criticism. The brethren present heard the voice, but no one saw the speaker. This was the sole ground for the belief that it was not a human utterance. Again, there is the arching of the fire round the martyr like a sail swelled by the wind (§ 15). But this may be explained as a strictly natural occurrence, and similar phenomena have been witnessed more than once on like occasions, notably at the martyrdoms of Savonarola and of Hooper. Again, there is the sweet scent, as of incense, issuing from the burning pyre (§ 15) ; but this phenomenon also, however we may explain it, whether from the fragrance of the wood or in some other way, meets us constantly. In another early record of martyrdoms, the history of the persecutions at Vienne and Lyons, a little more than twenty years later, we are told (Euseb. *H. E.* v. 1, § 35) that the heroic martyrs, as they stepped forward to meet their fate, were 'fragrant with the sweet odour of Christ, so that some persons even supposed that they had been anointed with material ointment' (ὥστε ἐνίους δόξαι καὶ μύρῳ κοσμικῷ κεχρίσθαι αὐτούς). Yet there was no pyre and no burning wood here, so that the imagination of the bystanders must have supplied the incident. Indeed, this account of the Gallican martyrs, indisputably written by eye-witnesses, contains many more startling occurrences than the record of Polycarp's fate.

"More or less closely connected with the miraculous element is the *prophetic insight* attributed to Polycarp. But what does this amount to ? It is stated indeed that 'every word which he uttered was accomplished and will be accomplished' (§ 16). But the future tense, 'will be accomplished,' is itself the expression of a belief, not the statement of a fact. We may, indeed, accept this qualification as clear testimony that, when the narrative was written, many of his forebodings and predictions had not been fulfilled. The only example of a prediction actually given in the narrative is the dream of his burning pillow, which suggested to him that he would undergo martyrdom by fire. But what more natural than this presentiment, when persecution was raging around him and fire was a common instrument of death ? I need not stop here to discuss how far a prescience may be vouchsafed to God's saints. Even ' old experience ' is found to be gifted with ' something like prophetic strain.' It is sufficient to say here again that it would be difficult to point to a single authentic biography of any Christian hero—certainly of any Christian hero of the early centuries—of whom some incident at least as remarkable as this prophecy, if prophecy it can be called, is not recorded.   Pontius, the disciple and biographer of Cyprian, relates a similar intimation which preceded the martyrdom of his master, and adds : ' Quid hac revelatione manifestius ? quid hac dignatione felicius ? ante illi prædicta sunt omnia quæcunque postmodum subsecuta sunt.' (*Vit. et Pass. Cypr.* 12, 13.)" [1]

I am the more anxious to quote this extract from a work, written long after the essays on *Supernatural Religion,* as it presents Dr. Lightfoot in a very different light, and gives me an opportunity of congratulating him on the apparent progress of his thought towards freedom which it exhibits.   I quite agree with him that the presence of supernatural or superstitious elements is no evidence against the authenticity of an early Christian writing, but the promptitude with which he sets these aside as interpolations, or explains them away into naturalism, is worthy of Professor Huxley. He now understands, without doubt, the reason why I demand such clear and conclusive evidence of miracles, and why I refuse to accept such narratives upon anonymous and insufficient testimony.   In fact, he cannot complain that I feel bound to explain all alleged miraculous occurrences precisely in the way of which he has set me so good an example, and that, whilst feeling nothing but very sympathetic appreciation of the emotion which stimulated the imagination and devout reverence of early Christians to such mistakes, I resolutely refuse to believe their pious aberrations.

[1] Lightfoot, *Apostolic Fathers,* part ii. 1885, p. 508 ff.

VIII.

CONCLUSIONS.

WE have seen that Divine Revelation could only be necessary or conceivable for the purpose of communicating to us something which we could not otherwise discover, and that the truth of communications which are essentially beyond and undiscoverable by reason cannot be attested in any other way than by miraculous signs distinguishing them as Divine. It is admitted that no other testimony could justify our believing the specific Revelation which we are considering, the very substance of which is supernatural and beyond the criticism of reason, and that its doctrines, if not proved to be miraculous truths, must inevitably be pronounced " the wildest delusions." " By no rational being could a just and benevolent life be accepted as proof of such astonishing announcements."

On examining the alleged miraculous evidence for Christianity as Divine Revelation, however, we find that, even if the actual occurrence of the supposed miracles could be substantiated, their value as evidence would be destroyed by the necessary admission that miracles are not limited to one source and are not exclusively associated with truth, but are performed by various spiritual Beings, Satanic as well as Divine, and are not always evidential, but are sometimes to be regarded as delusive and for the trial of faith. As the doctrines supposed to

be revealed are beyond Reason, and cannot in any sense
be intelligently approved by the human intellect, no
evidence which is of so doubtful and inconclusive a
nature could sufficiently attest them.   This alone would
disqualify the Christian miracles for the duty which
miracles alone are capable of performing.

The supposed miraculous evidence for the Divine
Revelation, moreover, is not only without any special
Divine character, being avowedly common also to
Satanic agency, but it is not original either in conception or details.   Similar miracles are reported long
antecedently to the first promulgation of Christianity,
and continued to be performed for centuries after it.
A stream of miraculous pretension, in fact, has flowed
through all human history, deep and broad as it has
passed through the darker ages, but dwindling down to
a thread as it has entered days of enlightenment.   The
evidence was too hackneyed and commonplace to make
any impression upon those before whom the Christian
miracles are said to have been performed, and it altogether failed to convince the people to whom the Revelation was primarily addressed.   The selection of such
evidence for such a purpose is much more characteristic
of human weakness than of Divine power.

The true character of miracles is at once betrayed
by the fact that their supposed occurrence has thus
been confined to ages of ignorance and superstition,
and that they are absolutely unknown in any time or
place where science has provided witnesses fitted to
appreciate and ascertain the nature of such exhibitions
of supernatural power.   There is not the slightest evidence that any attempt was made to investigate the
supposed miraculous occurrences, or to justify the inferences so freely drawn from them, nor is there any
reason to believe that the witnesses possessed, in any

considerable degree, the fulness of knowledge and
sobriety of judgment requisite for the purpose. No
miracle has yet established its claim to the rank even
of apparent reality, and all such phenomena must remain in the dim region of imagination. The test
applied to the largest class of miracles, connected with
demoniacal possession, discloses the falsity of all miraculous pretension.

There is no uncertainty as to the origin of belief in
supernatural interference with nature. The assertion
that spurious miracles have sprung up round a few
instances of genuine miraculous power has not a single
valid argument to support it. History clearly demonstrates that, wherever ignorance and superstition have
prevailed, every obscure occurrence has been attributed
to supernatural agency, and it is freely acknowledged
that, under their influence, ' inexplicable ' and ' miraculous ' are convertible terms. On the other hand, in proportion as knowledge of natural laws has increased, the
theory of supernatural interference with the order of
nature has been dispelled and miracles have ceased.
The effect of science, however, is not limited to the
present and future, but its action is equally retrospective,
and phenomena which were once ignorantly isolated
from the sequence of natural cause and effect are now
restored to their place in the unbroken order. Ignorance and superstition created miracles; knowledge
has for ever annihilated them.

To justify miracles, two assumptions are made: first,
an Infinite Personal God; and second, a Divine design
of Revelation, the execution of which necessarily involves supernatural action. Miracles, it is argued, are
not contrary to nature, or effects produced without
adequate causes, but on the contrary are caused by the
intervention of this Infinite Personal God for the pur-

pose of attesting and carrying out the Divine design. Neither of the assumptions, however, can be reasonably maintained.

The assumption of an Infinite Personal God : a Being at once limited and unlimited, is a use of language to which no mode of human thought can possibly attach itself. Moreover, the assumption of a God working miracles is emphatically excluded by universal experience of the order of nature. The allegation of a specific Divine cause of miracles is further inadequate from the fact that the power of working miracles is avowedly not limited to a Personal God, but is also ascribed to other spiritual Beings, and it must, consequently, always be impossible to prove that the supposed miraculous phenomena originate with one and not with the other. On the other hand, the assumption of a Divine design of Revelation is not suggested by antecedent probability, but is derived from the very Revelation which it is intended to justify, as is likewise the assumption of a Personal God, and both are equally vicious as arguments. The circumstances which are supposed to require this Divine design, and the details of the scheme, are absolutely incredible and opposed to all the results of science. Nature does not countenance any theory of the original perfection and subsequent degradation of the human race, and the supposition of a frustrated original plan of creation, and of later impotent endeavours to correct it, is as inconsistent with Divine omnipotence and wisdom as the proposed punishment of the human race and the mode devised to save some of them are opposed to justice and morality. Such assumptions are essentially inadmissible, and totally fail to explain and justify miracles.

Whatever definition be given of miracles, such exceptional phenomena must at least be antecedently incredible. In the absence of absolute knowledge, human belief must be guided by the balance of evidence, and it is obvious that the evidence for the uniformity of the order of nature, which is derived from universal experience, must be enormously greater than can be the testimony for any alleged exception to it. On the other hand, universal experience prepares us to consider mistakes of the senses, imperfect observation and erroneous inference as not only possible, but eminently probable on the part of the witnesses of phenomena, even when they are perfectly honest and truthful, and more especially so when such disturbing causes as religious excitement and superstition are present. When the report of the original witnesses only reaches us indirectly and through the medium of tradition, the probability of error is further increased. Thus the allegation of miracles is discredited, both positively by the invariability of the order of nature, and negatively by the fallibility of human observation and testimony. The history of miraculous pretension in the world and the circumstances attending the special exhibition of it which we are examining suggest natural explanations of the reported facts which wholly remove them from the region of the supernatural.

When we proceed to examine the direct witnesses for the Christian miracles, we do not discover any exceptional circumstances neutralising the preceding considerations. On the contrary, we find that the case turns not upon miracles substantially before us, but upon the mere narratives of miracles said to have occurred over eighteen hundred years ago. It is obvious that, for such narratives to possess any real force and validity, it is essential that their character and authorship should be placed beyond all doubt. They must proceed from eye-witnesses capable of estimating aright

M

the nature of the phenomena.   Our four Gospels, however, are strictly anonymous works.   The superscrip-
tions which now distinguish them are undeniably of
later origin than the works themselves and do not proceed from the composers of the Gospels.   Of the writers
to whom these narratives are traditionally ascribed
only two are even said to have been apostles, the alleged
authors of the second and third Synoptics neither having
been personal followers of Jesus nor eye-witnesses of
the events they describe.   Under these circumstances,
we are wholly dependent upon external evidence for
information regarding the authorship and trustworthiness of the four canonical Gospels.

In examining this evidence, we proceeded upon
clear and definite principles.   Without forming or
adopting any theory whatever as to the date or origin
of our Gospels, we simply searched the writings of the
Fathers, during a century and a half after the events
in question, for information regarding the composition
and character of these works and even for any certain
traces of their use, although, if discovered, these could
prove little beyond the mere existence of the Gospels
used at the date of the writer.   In the latter and minor
investigation, we were guided by canons of criticism,
previously laid down, which are based upon the simplest laws of evidence.   We found that the writings
of the Fathers, during a century and a half after the
death of Jesus, are a complete blank so far as any
evidence regarding the composition and character of
our Gospels is concerned, unless we except the tradition
preserved by Papias, after the middle of the second
century, the details of which fully justify the conclusion
that our first and second Synoptics, in their present
form, cannot be the works said to have been composed
by Matthew and Mark.   There is thus no evidence

whatever directly connecting any of the canonical Gospels with the writers to whom they are popularly attributed, and later tradition, of little or no value in itself, is separated by a long interval of profound silence from the epoch at which they are supposed to have been composed. With one exception, moreover, we found that, during the same century and a half, there is no certain and unmistakable trace even of the anonymous use of any of our Gospels in the early Church. This fact, of course, does not justify the conclusion that none of these Gospels was actually in existence during any part of that time, nor have we anywhere suggested such an inference, but strict examination of the evidence shows that there is no positive proof that they were. The exception to which we refer is Marcion's Gospel, which was, we think, based upon our third Synoptic, and consequently must be accepted as evidence of the existence of that work. Marcion, however, does not give the slightest information as to the authorship of the Gospel, and his charges against it of adulteration cannot be considered very favourable testimony as to its infallible character. The canonical Gospels continue to the end anonymous documents of no evidential value for miracles. They do not themselves pretend to be inspired histories, and they cannot escape from the ordinary rules of criticism. Internal evidence does not modify the inferences from external testimony. Apart from continual minor contradictions throughout the first three Gospels, it is impossible to reconcile the representations of the Synoptics with those of the fourth Gospel. They mutually destroy each other as evidence. They must be pronounced mere narratives compiled long after the events recorded, by unknown persons who were neither eyewitnesses of the alleged miraculous occurrences nor hearers of the statements they profess to report. They cannot be accepted as adequate testimony for miracles and the reality of Divine Revelation.

Applying similar tests to the Acts of the Apostles, we arrived at similar results. Acknowledged to be composed by the same author who produced the third Synoptic, that author's identity is not thereby made more clear. There is no evidence of the slightest value regarding its character, but, on the other hand, the work itself teems to such an extent with miraculous incidents and supernatural agency that the credibility of the narrative requires an extraordinary amount of attestation to secure for it any serious consideration. When the statements of the author are compared with the emphatic declarations of the Apostle Paul and with authentic accounts of the development of the early Christian Church, it becomes evident that the Acts of the Apostles, as might have been supposed, is a legendary composition of a later day, which cannot be regarded as sober and credible history, and rather discredits than tends to establish the reality of the miracles with which its pages so suspiciously abound.

The remaining books of the New Testament Canon required no separate examination, because, even if genuine, they contain no additional testimony to the reality of Divine Revelation, beyond the implied belief in such doctrines as the Incarnation and Resurrection. It is unquestionable, we suppose, that in some form or other the Apostles believed in these miracles, and the assumption that they did so supersedes the necessity for examining the authenticity of the Catholic Epistles and Apocalypse. In like manner, the recognition as genuine of four Epistles of Paul, which contain his testimony to miracles, renders it superfluous to discuss the authenticity of the other letters attributed to him.

The general belief in miraculous power and its possession by the Church is brought to a practical test in the case of the Apostle Paul. After elaborate consideration of his letters, we came to the unhesitating conclusion that, instead of establishing the reality of miracles, the unconscious testimony of Paul clearly demonstrates the facility with which erroneous inferences convert the most natural phenomena into supernatural occurrences.

As a final test, we carefully examined the whole of the evidence for the cardinal dogmas of Christianity, the Resurrection and Ascension of Jesus. First taking the four Gospels, we found that their accounts of these events are not only full of legendary matter, but even contradict and exclude each other and, so far from establishing the reality of such stupendous miracles, they show that no reliance is to be placed on the statements of the unknown authors. Taking next the testimony of Paul, which is more important as at least authentic and proceeding from an Apostle of whom we know more than of any other of the early missionaries of Christianity, we saw that it was indefinite and utterly insufficient. His so-called " circumstantial account of the testimony upon which the belief in the Resurrection rested " consists merely of vague and undetailed hearsay, differing, so far as it can be compared, from the statements in the Gospels, and without other attestation than the bare fact that it is repeated by Paul, who doubtless believed it, although he had not himself been a witness of any of the supposed appearances of the risen Jesus which he so briefly catalogues. Paul's own personal testimony to the Resurrection is limited to a vision of Jesus, of which we have no authentic details, seen many years after the alleged miracle. Considering the peculiar and highly nervous temperament of Paul,

of which he himself supplies abundant evidence, there
can be no hesitation in deciding that this vision was
purely subjective, as were likewise, in all probability,
the appearances to the excited disciples of Jesus. The
testimony of Paul himself, before his imagination was
stimulated to ecstatic fervour by the beauty of a spiritual-
ised religion, was an earnest denial of the great Christian
dogma, emphasised by the active persecution of those
who affirmed it; and a vision, especially in the case of
one so constituted, supposed to be seen many years
after the fact of the Resurrection had ceased to be
capable of verification, is not an argument of convincing
force. We were compelled to pronounce the evidence
for the Resurrection and Ascension absolutely and
hopelessly inadequate to prove the reality of such stupendous miracles, which must consequently be unhesi-
tatingly rejected. There is no reason given, or even
conceivable, why allegations such as these, and dogmas
affecting the religion and even the salvation of the
human race, should be accepted upon evidence which
would be declared totally insufficient in the case of any
common question of property or title before a legal tri-
bunal. On the contrary, the more momentous the point
to be established, the more complete must be the proof
required.

If we test the results at which we have arrived by
general considerations, we find them everywhere confirmed and established. There is nothing original in
the claim of Christianity to be regarded as Divine Revelation, and nothing new either in the doctrines said to
have been revealed, or in the miracles by which it is
alleged to have been distinguished. There has not been
a single historical religion largely held amongst men
which has not pretended to be divinely revealed, and
the written books of which have not been represented

as directly inspired. There is not a doctrine, sacrament, or rite of Christianity which has not substantially formed part of earlier religions ; and not a single phase of the supernatural history of the Christ, from his miraculous conception, birth and incarnation to his death, resurrection, and ascension, which has not had its counterpart in earlier mythologies. Heaven and hell, with characteristic variation of details, have held an important place in the eschatology of many creeds and races. The same may be said even of the moral teaching of Christianity, the elevated precepts of which, although in a less perfect and connected form, had already suggested themselves to many noble minds and been promulgated by ancient sages and philosophers. That this Enquiry into the reality of Divine Revelation has been limited to the claim of Christianity has arisen solely from a desire to condense it within reasonable bounds, and confine it to the only Religion in connection with which it could practically interest us now.

There is nothing in the history and achievements of Christianity which can be considered characteristic of a Religion Divinely revealed for the salvation of mankind. Originally said to have been communicated to a single nation, specially selected as the peculiar people of God, for whom distinguished privileges were said to be reserved, it was almost unanimously rejected by that nation at the time and it has continued to be repudiated by its descendants, with singular unanimity, to the present day. After more than eighteen centuries, this Divine scheme of salvation has not obtained even the nominal adhesion of more than a third of the human race, and if, in a census of Christendom, distinction could now be made of those who no longer seriously believe in it as Supernatural Religion, Christianity would take a much lower numerical position. Sâkya Muni, a teacher only second in nobility of character to Jesus, who, like him, proclaimed a system of elevated morality, has even now almost twice the number of followers, although his missionaries never sought converts in the West.[1] Considered as a scheme Divinely devised as the best, if not only, mode of redeeming the human race and saving them from eternal damnation, promulgated by God himself incarnate in human form, and completed by his own actual death upon the cross for the sins of the world, such results as these can only be regarded as practical failure, although they may not be disproportionate for a system of elevated morality.

We shall probably never be able to determine how far the great Teacher may through his own speculations or misunderstood spiritual utterances have suggested the supernatural doctrines subsequently attributed to him, and by which his whole history and system soon became transformed; but no one who attentively studies the subject can fail to be struck by the absence of such dogmas from the earlier records of his teaching. It is to the excited veneration of the followers of Jesus,

---

[1] By recent returns the number of the professors of different religions is estimated as follows :—

Parsees	.	.	150,000			
Sikhs	.	.	1,200,000			
Jews	.	.	7,000,000, being about	$\frac{1}{2}$	per cent. of the whole.	
Greek Catholics	.	75,000,000	,,	6	,,	,,
Roman Catholics	.	152,000,000	,,	12	,,	,,
Other Christians	.	100,000,000	,,	8	,,	,,
Hindus	.	.	160,000,000	,,	13	,,	,,
Muhammedans	.	.	155,000,000	,,	$12\frac{1}{2}$	,,	,,
Buddhists	.	.	500,000,000	,,	40	,,	,,
Not included in the above	.	. }	100,000,000	,,	8	,,	,,
			1,250,350,000			

We have taken these statistics, which are approximately correct, from an excellent little work recently published by the Society for the Propagation of Christian Knowledge—*Buddhism*, by T. W. Rhys Davids, p. 6.

however, that we owe most of the supernatural elements so characteristic of the age and people. We may look in vain even in the synoptic Gospels for the doctrines elaborated in the Pauline Epistles and the Gospel of Ephesus. The great transformation of Christianity was effected by men who had never seen Jesus, and who were only acquainted with his teaching after it had become transmuted by tradition. The fervid imagination of the East constructed Christian theology. It is not difficult to follow the development of the creeds of the Church, and it is certainly most instructive to observe the progressive boldness with which its dogmas were expanded by pious enthusiasm. The New Testament alone represents several stages of dogmatic evolution. Before his first followers had passed away the process of transformation had commenced. The disciples, who had so often misunderstood the teaching of Jesus during his life, piously distorted it after his death. His simple lessons of meekness and humility were soon forgotten. With lamentable rapidity, the elaborate structure of ecclesiastical Christianity, following stereotyped lines of human superstition and deeply coloured by Alexandrian philosophy, displaced the sublime morality of Jesus. Doctrinal controversy, which commenced amongst the very Apostles, has ever since divided the unity of the Christian body. The perverted ingenuity of successive generations of churchmen has filled the world with theological quibbles, which have naturally enough culminated of late in doctrines of Immaculate Conception and Papal Infallibility.

It is sometimes affirmed, however, that those who proclaim such conclusions not only wantonly destroy the dearest hopes of humanity, but remove the only solid basis of morality; and it is alleged that, before existing belief is disturbed, the iconoclast is bound to provide a substitute for the shattered idol. To this we may reply that speech or silence does not alter the reality of things. The recognition of Truth cannot be made dependent on consequences, or be trammelled by considerations of spurious expediency. Its declaration in a serious and suitable manner to those who are capable of judging can never be premature. Its suppression cannot be effectual, and is only a humiliating compromise with conscious imposture. In so far as morality is concerned, belief in a system of future rewards and punishments, although of an intensely degraded character, may, to a certain extent, have promoted observance of the letter of the law in darker ages and even in our own; but it may, we think, be shown that education and civilisation have done infinitely more to enforce its spirit. How far Christianity has promoted education and civilisation, we shall not here venture adequately to discuss. We may emphatically assert, however, that whatever beneficial effect Christianity has produced has been due, not to its supernatural dogmas, but to its simple morality. Dogmatic Theology, on the contrary, has retarded education and impeded science. Wherever it has been dominant, civilisation has stood still. Science has been judged and suppressed by the light of a text or a chapter of Genesis. Almost every great advance which has been made towards enlightenment has been achieved in spite of the protest or the anathema of the Church. Submissive ignorance, absolute or comparative, has been tacitly fostered as the most desirable condition of the popular mind. " Except ye be converted, and become as little children, ye shall not enter into the kingdom of heaven," has been the favourite text of Doctors of Divinity with a stock of incredible dogmas difficult of assimilation by the virile mind. Even now, the friction of theological resistance is a constant waste of intellectual power. The early enunciation of so pure a system of morality, and one so intelligible to the simple as well as profound to the wise, was of great value to the world ; but, experience being once systematised and codified, if higher principles do not constrain us, society may safely be left to see morals sufficiently observed. It is true that, notwithstanding its fluctuating rules, morality has hitherto assumed the character of a Divine institution, but its sway has not, in consequence, been more real than it must be as the simple result of human wisdom and the outcome of social experience. The choice of a noble life is no longer a theological question, and ecclesiastical patents of truth and uprightness have finally expired. Morality, which has ever changed its complexion and modified its injunctions according to social requirements, will necessarily be enforced as part of human evolution, and is not dependent on religious terrorism or superstitious persuasion. If we are disposed to say : *Cui bono?* and only practise morality, or be ruled by right principles, to gain a heaven or escape a hell, there is nothing lost, for such grudging and calculated morality is merely a spurious imitation which can as well be produced by social compulsion. But if we have ever been really penetrated by the pure spirit of morality, if we have in any degree attained that elevation of mind which instinctively turns to the true and noble and shrinks from the baser level of thought and action, we shall feel no need of the stimulus of a system of rewards and punishments in a future state which has for so long been represented as essential to Christianity.

As to the other reproach, let us ask what has actually been destroyed by such an enquiry pressed to its logical conclusion. Can Truth by any means be made less true ? Can reality be melted into thin air ? The

Revelation not being a reality, that which has been destroyed is only an illusion, and that which is left is the Truth. Losing belief in it and its contents, we have lost absolutely nothing but that which the traveller loses when the mirage, which has displayed cool waters and green shades before him, melts swiftly away. There were no cool fountains really there to allay his thirst, no flowery meadows for his wearied limbs; his pleasure was delusion, and the wilderness is blank. Rather the mirage with its pleasant illusion, is the human cry, than the desert with its barrenness. Not so, is the friendly warning; seek not vainly in the desert that which is not there, but turn rather to other horizons and to surer hopes. Do not waste life clinging to ecclesiastical dogmas which represent no eternal verities, but search elsewhere for truth which may haply be found. What should we think of the man who persistently repulsed the persuasion that two and two make four from the ardent desire to believe that two and two make five? Whose fault is it that two and two do make four and not five? Whose folly is it that it should be more agreeable to think that two and two make five than to know that they only make four? This folly is theirs who represent the value of life as dependent on the reality of special illusions, which they have religiously adopted. To discover that a former belief is unfounded is to change nothing of the realities of existence. The sun will descend as it passes the meridian whether we believe it to be noon or not. It is idle and foolish, if human, to repine because the truth is not precisely what we thought it, and at least we shall not change reality by childishly clinging to a dream.

The argument so often employed by theologians that Divine Revelation is necessary for man, and that certain views contained in that Revelation are required by our moral consciousness, is purely imaginary and derived from the Revelation which it seeks to maintain. The only thing absolutely necessary for man is Truth ; and to that, and that alone, must our moral consciousness adapt itself. Reason and experience forbid the expectation that we can acquire any knowledge otherwise than through natural channels. We might as well expect to be supernaturally nourished as supernaturally informed. To complain that we do not know all that we desire to know is foolish and unreasonable. It is tantamount to complaining that the mind of man is not differently constituted. To attain the full altitude of the Knowable, whatever that may be, should be our earnest aim, and more than this is not for humanity. We may be certain that information which is beyond the ultimate reach of Reason is as unnecessary as it is inaccessible. Man may know all that man requires to know.

We gain more than we lose by awaking to find that our Theology is human invention and our eschatology an unhealthy dream. We are freed from the incubus of base Hebrew mythology, and from doctrines of Divine government which outrage morality and set cruelty and injustice in the place of holiness. If we have to abandon cherished anthropomorphic visions of future Blessedness, the details of which are either of unseizable dimness or of questionable joy, we are at least delivered from quibbling discussions of the meaning of αἰώνιος, and our eternal hope is unclouded by the doubt whether mankind is to be tortured in hell for ever and a day, or for a day without the ever. At the end of life there may be no definite vista of a Heaven glowing with the light of apocalyptic imagination, but neither will there be the unutterable horror of a Purgatory or a Hell lurid with flames for the helpless victims of an unjust but omnipotent Creator. To entertain such libellous representations at all as part of the contents of " Divine Revelation," it was necessary to assert that man was incompetent to judge of the ways of the God of Revelation, and must not suppose him endowed with the perfection of human conceptions of justice and mercy, but submit to call wrong right and right wrong at the foot of an almighty Despot. But now the reproach of such reasoning is shaken from our shoulders, and returns to the Jewish superstition from which it sprang.

As myths lose their might and their influence when discovered to be baseless, the power of supernatural Christianity will doubtless pass away, but the effect of the revolution must not be exaggerated, although it cannot here be fully discussed. If the pictures which have filled for so long the horizon of the Future must vanish, no hideous blank can rightly be maintained in their place. We should clearly distinguish between what we know and know not, but as carefully abstain from characterising that which we know not as if it were really known to us. That mysterious Unknown or Unknowable is no cruel darkness, but simply an impenetrable distance into which we are impotent to glance, but which excludes no legitimate speculation and forbids no reasonable hope.

INDEX.

ACT

Acts of the Apostles, evidence for, 142 f., 164
Addai, Doctrine of, 147
Ammonius, *Diatessaron* of, 148
Anger, 5
Antioch, earthquake at, in A.D. 115, 107 f.
Aphthonius; see Elias of Salamia
Apocalypse, allusion to Paul in, 26, n. 2; language of, 27 ff.
Apollinaris, Claudius; date, 137; evidence for Gospels, 137
Aristion, 55
Ascension, evidence for, 165
Aubertin, 65, 66
Aucher, 145

Baronius, 112 n.
Bar-Salibi, Dionysius, 147 f.
Basnage, 65, 66
Baumgarten-Crusius, 70, 72
Baur, does not allude to Armenian version of Ignatian Epistles, 79; date of martyrdom of Ignatius, 89 f.; place of his martyrdom, 95 ff.; on Peregrinus Proteus, 102
Beausobre, 70, 71
Bleek, 7, 32, 60, 62, 63, 74, 80, 90, 93
Blondel, 65, 66
Bochart, 65, 66
Böhringer, 59, 62, 63, 80
Bunsen, 32, 62, 63, 79

Calvin, 64
Campianus, 64

DIA

Casaubon, 65, 67
Celsus, Origen on, 10 ff., 146
Centuriators, Magdeburg, 64
Chemnitz, 62, 64, 65
Christianity, claim to be Divine Revelation, not original, 166 f.; history and achievements opposed to this claim, 167 f.; census of religions, 168 n. 1; transformation of, 169 f.
Chrysostom, 108, 110, 111 f.
Ciasca, alleged Arabic version of Tatian's *Diatessaron*, 145, 150 f.
Clement of Alexandria, on Basilides, 18 f.
Cleophas, 52
Cook, 65, 66
Criticism, attitude towards, 1
Cureton, 62, 63, 65, 68 ff., 79, 83 f.
Curetonian version of Ignatian Epistles, 59 ff., 67 ff., 74 ff., 80 f.

Dallæus, 62
Davidson, Dr., on passage of Irenæus, 6; date of martyrdom of Ignatius, 91; place of the martyrdom, 96
Delitzsch, 30, 31, 32
Denzinger, 78, 79, 80 n. 2, 103 n. 1
Diatessaron of Ammonius, 148 ff., 152 ff.
Diatessaron of Elias of Salamia, 148 ff.
Diatessaron of Tatian, 145 ff.; alleged Armenian version of Ephraem's commentary on it, 145 f.; Latin translation by

DIO

Aucher and Moesinger, 145 f.; Arabic version of, translated by Ciasca, 145 f.; Eusebius on it, 146 f.; did Eusebius directly know it? 146 f.; Bar-Salibi on it, 147 f.; Theodoret suppresses it, 149 f.; the genealogies of Jesus said to be excised, 149 f.; not all suppressed in Armenian and Arabic works, 150; called 'Gospel according to the Hebrews,' 150; Epiphanius had not seen it, 150; we could not identify it, 150; Arabic version of Ciasca, 150 f.; said to be translated from Syriac, 151; its date, 151; ascribed in notes to Tatian, 151; original language of Tatian's *Diatessaron*, 151 f.; Gospel texts in alleged versions affected by repeated translation, 151 f.; name of Tatian not on original work, 152; could it be identified? 152 ff.; case of Victor of Capua, 152 ff.; was he mistaken? 153 f.; Dr. Wace says: No, 153; value of evidence if alleged versions be genuine, 154

Dionysius of Corinth, 56

Doctrine of Addai, 147

Donaldson, Dr., on Epistle of Polycarp, 21; on Tatian's *Diatessaron*, 150

Dorner, 4

Dressel, 79 f.

EBRARD, 7

Elias of Salamia, his *Diatessaron*, 147 f.; he finds fault with Canons of Eusebius, 148

Ephraem Syrus, his Commentary on Tatian's *Diatessaron*, 147 f.; date, 148; alleged Armenian version of his Commentary, 145; date of the MS., 150; translated from Syriac, 150; evidence, 150 f.; Tatian's name not mentioned, 150; value as evidence if genuine, 154

Epiphanius, 150

Eusebius, on Papias, 7; silence of, 45 f.; my only inference from silence of, 50 f.; procedure of,

GUE

50 f.; his references to Hegesippus, 52 ff.; his references to John, 53 ff.; on Claudius Apollinaris, 137; on Polycrates of Ephesus, 137; on Tatian's *Diatessaron*, 146 f.; on *Diatessaron* of Ammonius, 148 f.; his Epistle to Carpianus, 148 f., 152

Ewald, 32, 33, 62, 63, 79, 141

FARRAR, Dr., 34

Francke, 97

GFRÖRER, 7, 75

Glaucias, 15, 18, 19

Gobarus, Stephanus, 23

Godet, 32

Gospel, the Fourth, contrast with Synoptics, 26 f., 26 n. 2; Hebraic character of its language, 27 ff.; Eusebius regarding it, 49, 51, 53 f., 55 ff.; evidence to it of Martyrdom of Polycarp, 135; alleged evidence of Claudius Apollinaris, 137; alleged evidence of Polycrates, 137; supposed reference to it in Epistle of Vienne and Lyons, 144; Tatian's *Diatessaron* said to begin with it, 147 f.; insufficiency of evidence for it, 162 ff.; its contents cannot be reconciled with Synoptics, 163 f.

Gospels, Justin's use of, 24 f.; evidence of alleged quotations, 24 f.; object in examining evidence for, 37 ff., 41 ff.; numerous Gospels circulating in early Church, 131 f.; anonymous quotations not necessarily from canonical, 131 ff.; illustrations of this, 132 ff.; evidence of Martyrdom of Polycarp, 135; evidence of Melito of Sardis, 135 f.; evidence of Claudius Apollinaris, 137; evidence of Epistle of Vienne and Lyons, 141 ff.; principles on which evidence is examined, 162; insufficiency of evidence for, 162 ff.

Groot, Hofstede de, 5, 9 n. 2

Grove, 34

Guericke, 7, 90 f., 93

HAD

HADRIAN, 12
Hagenbach, 91, 93
Harless, 75
Hase, 76
Hebrews, Gospel according to the,
122 f., 123, 150
Hefele, 80
Hegesippus, his attitude to Paul,
23 ; references to him by Eusebius, 52 ff. ; on Simeon, 52
Hemphill, Professor, did Eusebius
directly know Tatian's *Diates-
saron* ? 146 f. ; on Arabic *Dia-
tessaron*, 149 ; it takes Matthew
as basis, 149 ; its substantial
identity with Victor's *Diates-
saron*, 158
Hengstenberg, 31
Hilgenfeld, on passage of Irenæus,
5 f. ; on Ignatian Epistles, 78, 79 ;
place and date of martyrdom of
Ignatius, 97 ff. ; on Papias and
Matthew's Hebrew "Oracles,"
122 ; Protevangelium Jacobi,
142 ; Eusebius on Tatian's *Diatessaron*, 146 f.
Hippolytus, 17 f.
Holtzmann, 135, 147
Hug, 32
Humfrey, 66

IGNATIUS, Epistle of Polycarp regarding him, 20 ff. ; date and
place of his martyrdom, 87 ff.,
94 ff. ; his alleged martyr-journey,
94 ff. ; his treatment during it,
99 f. ; compared with Paul's journey, 100 f. ; compared with case
of Peregrinus, 101 ff. ; reasons
opposed to martyr-journey to
Rome, and for martyrdom in Antioch, 104 ff. ; remains of Ignatius, 111 ff ; martyrologies, 112 f.
Ignatian Epistles, Dr. Lightfoot on,
57 ff. ; critics on priority of Syriac version, 59 ff. ; long recension, 64 ff. ; Vossian Epistles,
67 ff. ; version of Ussher, 67 ;
Armenian version, 78 ff. ; Euse-
bian Epistles, 80 ff. ; their order
in MSS., 82 ff. ; their value as
evidence, 113 f.
Irenæus, 3 ff.

LIG

JACOBSON, 65
Jerome, 110 f.
John, references of Eusebius, 53 ff. ;
Papias and Presbyters on, 55 f. ;
double use of name, 55 f.
Justin Martyr, his quotations, 23 ff.

KEIM, 135
Kestner, 70, 71
Kirchhofer, 7

LANGE, 32
Lardner, 70, 136
Lechler, 76 f.
Lightfoot, 32, 33
Lightfoot, Dr., objectionable style
of criticism, 1 f., 3, 7 f., 13 n. 1,
14 f., 15 n. 1, 20, 21, 23 f., 24 n. 5,
25 f., 27, 80 f., 36, 44 f., 46 f.,
57 ff., 68 ff., 73 ff., 144 ; on a passage of Irenæus, 3 ff. ; discussion
of date of Celsus, 9 ff. ; Dr. Westcott on Basilides, 15 ff. ; weightier
arguments of apologists, 20 ff. ;
on Epistle of Polycarp, 20 f. ;
object of Papias' work, 22 ; on
Hegesippus and Apostle Paul,
22 f. ; on Justin Martyr's quotations, 23 ff. ; on duration of ministry of Jesus, 26 f. ; on Hebraic
character of language of the
Fourth Gospel, 27 ff. ; identification of Sychar, 30 ff. ; on argument of S. R., 36 ff. ; on silence
of Eusebius, 45 ff. ; the intention
of Eusebius, 44 f. ; procedure of
Eusebius, 50 f. ; silence of Eusebius as evidence for Fourth Gospel, 56 f ; on Ignatian Epistles,
57 ff. ; on view of Lipsius, 60 f. ;
misstatements regarding references in S. R., 61 ff. ; differentia-
tion of Ignatian Epistles, 80 ff. ;
their position in MSS., 82 ff. ; on
martyr-journey and treatment of
Ignatius, 99 f. ; compared with
Apostle Paul's, 100 f. ; compared
with case of Peregrinus Proteus,
101 ff. ; on John Malalas, 108 ff. ;
on Polycarp of Smyrna, 115 f. ;
date of his Epistle, 115 ; does not
examine alleged quotations of

LIP

Gospels, 116 ; on Papias of Hierapolis, 117 ff. ; Papias on Mark,
117 f.; Papias on Matthew,
119 ff. ; on accuracy of Papias,
120 ff. ; translation of Hebrew
Oracles of Matthew, 121 f. ; on
Gospel according to the Hebrews,
122 f. ; on nature of Oracles of
Matthew, 124 ff. ; can Oracles
include narrative ? 125 f. ; his
misapprehension of argument of
S. R., 129 ff. ; on Martyrdom of
Polycarp, 135 ; on Melito of Sardis, 135 f. ; erroneous quotation
from S. R., 136 n. 2 ; on Claudius Apollinaris, 137 f. ; on Polycrates of Ephesus, 137 ; on Epistle of Vienne and Lyons, 139 ff. ;
on the "testimony of Zacharias,"
140 ff. ; alleged reference to
Acts, 142 f. ; alleged reference
to Fourth Gospel, 144 ; Tatian's
Diatessaron, 145 f. ; on Eusebius's mention of it, 146 f. ; did
he directly know it ? 146 ; on
Doctrine of Addai, 147 ; it mentions Tatian's *Diatessaron*, 147 ;
Dionysius Bar-Salibi on Tatian's
Diatessaron, 147 f. ; on *Diatessaron* of Ammonius, 148 ; quite
different from Tatian's work,
148 f. ; similarity to Arabic version asserted by Hemphill, 149 ;
case of Victor of Capua, 152 f. ;
Victor must have been mistaken,
153 f. ; Victor not mistaken after
all, 153 ; on Létter of the Smyrnaens, 154 ff. ; a short way with
its miraculous elements, 154 f. ;
practically justifies procedure of
" Supernatural Religion," 156
Lipsius, on Ignatian Epistles, 60 f.,
63, 78, 79 ; on Martyrdom of
Polycarp, 135
λόγια, meaning of, in N. T.,
124 ff.
Logos doctrine in Apocalypse, 30
n. 1
Lucian, 12, 101 f.
Luke, Gospel according to, supposed reference to it in Epistle
of Vienne and Lyons, 141 f. ; its
use in *Diatessaron*, 149, 153
Luthardt, on passage of Irenæus,

PAP

6 ; on Basilides, 18 ; on language
of Fourth Gospel and Apocalypse,
28 ff.

Magdeburg Centuriators, 64
Malalas, John, on martyrdom of
Ignatius, 108 ff.
Marcus Aurelius, 105 f.
Mark, Presbyters and Papias on,
117 f. ; not eye-witness but inter-
preter of Peter, 118 f. ; value of
his Gospel as evidence, 118 f. ;
use in *Diatessaron*, 149
Matthew, Presbyters and Papias
on, 55 f., 119 ff. ; wrote oracles
in Hebrew, 119 ff. ; when trans-
lated, 121 ff. ; use in *Diatessaron*
of Ammonius, 148 ; also in that
of Tatian, 149 f.
Matthias, 16, 18
Mayerhoff, 91, 93
Melito of Sardis, 135 f.
Merx, 78, 79
Meyer, on passage of Irenæus, 5,
32
Mill, on miracles, 36 ff.
Milman, 59, 62, 63, 105 n. 1, 107 f.
Moesinger,Ephraem'sCommentary,
145 f., 150
Mozley, on belief, 35 f.

Neander, 70, 71 f., 105 f.
Neubauer, 30, 34
Nicephorus, 111 n. 1

Olshausen, 7, 32
" Oracles," meaning of, 124 ff.
Origen, on Celsus, 10 f.

Papias of Hierapolis, alleged quotations from him, 3 ff. ; object of
his work, 22 ; references of Eusebius to him, 54 ff. ; words of
the Presbyters, 55 f. ; double
reference to " John," 55 f. ; he
had nothing to tell of Fourth
Gospel, 55 ff. ; on Mark's Gospel,
117 ff. ; on Matthew's Hebrew
Oracles, 119 f. ; value of his evidence for the Gospels, 127 f.

PAR

Parker, 65, 66

Paul, Apostle, his treatment as prisoner compared to that of Ignatius, 100 f.; unconscious testimony regarding the supernatural, 165; his testimony for Resurrection and Ascension, 165 f.

Pearson, 67

Peregrinus Proteus, 102 ff.

Perpetua, Saturus and, 100

Petau, 65, 67

Petermann, 78 ff.

Phillips, 147

Polycarp of Smyrna, 115 f.; date of martyrdom, 115

Polycarp, Martyrdom of, 135, 154 ff.; Dr. Lightfoot's short way with the miraculous elements, 154 f.

Polycrates of Ephesus, date, 137; evidence for Fourth Gospel, 137

Pressensé, de, 60

Protevangelium Jacobi, 142

QUADRATUS, Statius, date of proconsulship, 115

" RELIGION, Supernatural," argument of, 36 ff., 40 ff., 129 ff.; canons of criticism, 130 ff.; the "testimony of Zacharias," Epistle of Vienne and Lyons, 140 ff.; was Eusebius directly acquainted with Tatian's *Diatessaron*? 146 f.; argument of S. R. practically justified by Dr. Lightfoot, 154 ff.; conclusions of, 157 ff.; evidence of Divine Revelation which is necessary, 157; miracles as evidence destroyed by doubtful source, 157 f.; miraculous evidence not original, 158 f.; stream of miraculous pretension, 158; true character of miracles betrayed, 158 f.; origin of belief in supernatural interference, 159; assumptions to justify miracles, 159 f.; an Infinite Personal God, 159 f.; Divine design of Revelation, 160; miracles antecedently incredible, 160 f.; evidence for the Christian miracles, 161 f.;

SYN

principles upon which evidence examined, 162; evidence for Gospels, 162 f.; evidence for Acts, 164; the remaining books of New Testament, 164 f.; evidence of Paul, 165; evidence for Resurrection and Ascension, 165 f.; results tested by general considerations, 166 ff.; claim of Christianity to be Divinely revealed not original, 166 f.; history and achievements of Christianity opposed to it, 167 f.; census of religions, 168 n. 1; how far the Great Teacher was misunderstood, 168 f.; transformation of Christianity, 169 f.; alleged objections to disturbing belief, 169 f.; objections not valid, 170 f.; argument that Divine Revelation is necessary to man, 172 f.; we gain more than we lose by finding our theology to be mere human inventions, 173 f.

Resurrection, evidence for, 165 f.

Reuss, 147

Riggenbach, on passage of Irenæus, 5; on Sychar, 82

Ritschl, 62, 63

Rivet, 64, 65, 67

Routh, on passage of Irenæus, 4

Ruinart, anniversary of Ignatius, 112

Rumpf, 60

SANDAY, 88

Saumaise, 65, 66

Schleimann, 75 f.

Scholten, 11 n. 2, 80, 91 f., 96 f., 147

Schrœckh, 70, 71

Schürer, 135

Shechem, 80 ff.

Simeon, 52, 105 f.

Smyrnaens, Letter of, 154 ff.; Dr. Lightfoot as a sceptical critic, 154 f.

Socinus, 65

Stephen, 142 f.

Sychar, 80 ff.

Synoptics, contrasted with Fourth Gospel, 26 f.

TAT

TATIAN'S *Diatessaron* : see Diatessaron

Theodoret, the Ignatian Epistles, 81

Thiersch, 7, 70

Tholuck, 7

Tischendorf, on passage of Irenæus, 3 ff.; passage of Celsus, 11 ff.; does not notice Armenian version of Ignatian Epistles, 80; "testimony of Zacharias," in Epistle of Vienne and Lyons, 142; it is a reference to the Protevangelium Jacobi, 142

Trajan, in connection with the martyrdom of Ignatius, 89 ff., 105 ff.

Tregelles, 60, 82 f.

UHLHORN, 78, 79

Ussher, 67

VIENNE and Lyons, Epistle of, 139 ff.; date, 139; the "testimony of Zacharias," 140 f.; alleged quotations of Acts, 142 ff.; value of evidence, 143; Dr. Lightfoot on fragrance of the martyrs, 155

Volkmar, on Celsus, 10 ff.; on Ignatian Epistles, 60; does not notice Armenian version, 80;

ZEL

date of martyrdom of Ignatius, 92 f.; place of martyrdom, 94 ff.

Vossian Epistles of Ignatius, 67 f.

WACE, Dr., 153

Waddington, 115

Weiss, 62, 63, 78, 79

Weissmann, 69 f.

Westcott, Dr., criticisms on, 3 f.; on Papias, 4; on Basilides, 15 ff.; on Justin Martyr's quotations, 23 ff.; on "Supernatural Religion," 44 f.; misstatements regarding notes, 85 ff.; was Eusebius directly acquainted with Tatian's *Diatessaron*? 147

Wette, de, 7, 15 n. 1, 82

Wieseler, 31, 32

Wotton, 68, 69

ZACHARIAS, the testimony of, Epistle of Vienne and Lyons, 140 ff.

Zahn, on passage of Irenæus, 6; on Ignatian Epistles, 78, 79, 99 n. 1, 101; on John Malalas, 110; date of martyrdom of Ignatius, 112; did Eusebius directly know Tatian's *Diatessaron*? 147; passages regarding descent of Jesus from David not all excised from alleged Armenian version, 150

Zeller, on passage of Irenæus, 5

PRINTED BY
SPOTTISWOODE AND CO., NEW-STREET SQUARE
LONDON

www.ingramcontent.com/pod-product-compliance
Lightning Source LLC
Chambersburg PA
CBHW030604040726
47497CB00008B/2849